DES DILLON was born and brought up in Coatbridge, Lanarkshire, and studied English at Strathclyde University. A former teacher, he is now a poet, short story writer, novelist and dramatist writing for radio, stage, television and film. He has taught Creative Writing at the Arvon Foundation and was Writer in Residence at Castlemilk, Glasgow, between 1998 and 2000. Des now lives in Galloway.

To date he is the author of eight novels and one poetry collection. His novel *Me and Ma Gal* was shortlisted for the Saltire Society Scottish First Book of the Year Award and won the 2003 World Book Day 'We Are What We Read' poll for the novel that best describes Scotland today. It was broadcast as a drama on Radio 4 in 2004. In 2003 his play *Lockerbie 103* went on national tour. *Six Black Candles* won the International Festival of Playwriting Award in 2001, and in 2004 played at the Royal Lyceum Theatre in Edinburgh, winning the Best Ensemble Award at the Critics' Awards for Theatre in Scotland. His latest play, *Monks*, is to receive its world premiere at the Royal Lyceum Theatre in Edinburgh.

Also by Des Dillon:

Fiction
Me and Ma Gal (1995)
The Big Empty: A Collection of Short Stories (1996)
Duck (1998)
Itchycooblue (1999)
Return of the Busby Babes (2000)
The Big Q (2001)
The Glasgow Dragon (2004)
Singin I'm No A Billy He's A Tim (2006)

Poetry
Picking Brambles (2003)

They Scream When You Kill Them

DES DILLON

Luath Press Limited

EDINBURGH

www.luath.co.uk

First published 2006

ISBN (10): 1-905222-35-1
ISBN (13): 978-1-905222-35-3

The author's right to be identified as author of this book
under the Copyright, Designs and Patents Act 1988 has been asserted.

The paper used in this book is recyclable. It is made from low-chlorine pulps
produced in a low-energy, low-emission manner from renewable forests.

The publisher acknowledges subsidy from

Scottish
Arts Council

towards the publication of this volume.

Printed and bound by
Bookmarque, Croydon, Surrey

Typeset in 9.5 point Frutiger

This collection is dedicated to the memory of cousin and pal
Jim Davis, who died in March 2006.
On ye go the Seamus!

Acknowledgements

Thanks to the SAC for the Writers' award that made the writing of these short stories possible. Not to mention two novels and another collection of short stories. On that note let the reader be warned that I ended up writing a novel, *My Epileptic Lurcher*, based on the following short stories: I Thought You'd Give Me Pills, Pink River, Saturne Monsieur and They Scream When You Kill Them. I have also developed Echo into a novel while The Blue Hen has already been developed and published by Sandstone Press as a novella.

Some of these stories have been published or broadcast before: Soap Opera was published in *Eildon Tree* (2006). He Ain't Heavy in *800 words* (2006). Big Brother on Radio 4 (2002). The Blue Hen in *New British Writing 10*; *Barcelona Review* in French, Spanish, Catalan and English; also broadcast on Radio 4. Darwin The Wise Old Space Elephant broadcast on Radio Scotland (2000). Echo broadcast on Radio Scotland (2005) and published in *Barcelona Review* (2005). Heatherstone's Question published in *The Scotsman* (1998) and in the collection *The Hope That Kills Us* (2002). Saturne Monsieur was published in *Gargoyle USA* 50th celebratory edition. They Scream When You Kill Them was published in *Freedom Spring* (2005).

Contents

Soap Opera

The reason I'm writing this is that tonight it all came back to me. That girl and that disagreement. I was in soap opera and had a stand off with this young and beautiful script editor. She said people wanted arguments to be over quickly and wanted me to cut a scene where the whole bar was watching a couple fight. She spouted some Psychology 101 theory about how our brains were wired to want fights to be over. I said it was entertainment.

—But it's not true to life, she said.

—I mean in real life – in a real bar – it's entertainment when an argument breaks out.

She dismissed that with a look, a Really and a London accent. I dug my heels in and they sacked me. That was five years ago.

So tonight I was in Bridgeton and I noticed a good kebab shop. It wasn't raining but it was one of them winter nights where there's a film of water on everything. A film that won't go away and leaves the world looking cold and heartless. The gutters had a few dark puddles for buses to splash in. My favourite puddle said kebab in neon mirror language. I splashed it into oblivion going in.

I had to shout over the top of the techno beat. Chemical Brothers.

—Spicy chicken kebab poke of chips can of coke please.

—Large?

—Aye.

—Salad?

—Aye cheers.

—Chilli sauce?

—Cheers mate.

The young guy bounced up and down to the music everything he done. Cutting the meat. Heating the pitta. Lifting the salad. He took my money and I read three days ago's *Sun*. I checked out the soap operas and the stories were the same as ever. Jack finds Laura in bed with Jean. Jan's long lost father comes back – as her boyfriend. Gangsters take over the local bar. The doctor becomes a junkie.

—Spicy chicken kebab chilli sauce poke of chips can of coke.

—Cheers mate.

He went back to his bobbing up and down and I walked out to a big argument across the street. A couple of dozen people at the bus stop were watching this argument. I slipped into the queue. This young guy about twenty-three was going at it hammer and tongs with a girl. He was well built with weights and had dark hair and good biceps. Good looking. The car and his age and the gold they were both wearing said drug dealer. She was tall, blonde and tanned and had her belly button pierced. I knew she'd been in the car cos on a cold night like this nobody was walking about Glasgow dressed like that. She had sandals on too. White sandals.

She kept walking away and he kept pulling her back. His car, a black BMW worth thirty grand, was purring at the side of the road with the driver's door flung open. There was techno music coming out of that too. I glanced in at the kebab guy and he was still bobbing and weaving with the Chemical Brothers. Bang! She slapped him this girl. The bus stop took a breath. If they'd been on their own he'd've slapped her back. But he couldn't out here with the whole world watching.

—Good slap, said the woman next to me.

I agreed with a slight nod and an 'mm hmm'. Although everybody was watching the entertainment none of us had our head facing directly across. He was the kind of guy that could turn on anybody. At any moment. None of us was giving him an excuse. By now they were close enough to hear what they were saying. She went to slap him again. He ducked and caught her hand. He ducked with such grace I thought he must be a boxer. Not a drug dealer.

—Get in the fuckin car, he shouted.

—What? In the seat where she was!?

Ah! We all knew now what it was about now.

—I only gave her a fuckin lift.

—Aye!

—Ask her, here ask her. He was holding out his mobile phone.

When the phone landed near us after bouncing and skimming across the road nobody looked like picking it up. He stared at it then scanned the bus stop but all he seen was people waiting on a bus. People inspecting the stones in the roadside or the high red clouds moving over the city. In the country, at night, they'd be black the clouds. But over a city they are always red. Like a beacon. Or a warning.

—Look what ye done to my phone, he said, like she'd killed it.

—Fuck your phone, she said. She was marching towards

3

him slapping with the ineffectual half-slaps girls like this are expert at. She looked like she was slapping her way through a flock of sparrows. He went backwards and the way he fended off the slaps confirmed he must be a boxer. Maybe that's what it is, I thought. He's not a drug dealer. He's a boxer. And he's up and coming. Made a few quid. Bought a nice car. And this is his bird. The one he's been seeing since before his rise through the ranks. But now some other, posher, more beautiful girl, had her gold-digging claws into him. Not that the sparrow-slapper wasn't beautiful. She was, but she'd lost this guy; you could see that. That was my surmisation of the story. But it could all change. It could all change in an instant.

She reached the car and started kicking the panels. He wrapped his arms round her lifting her off the ground. But she put two feet on the car and shoved them both backwards. He landed on his back in a cold puddle with her on top. Her skirt was up her arse and her knickers were white like her sandals. When she got up her knees and hands were dirty as if she'd been crawling about looking for something. There was a crash and the bus stop got a fright. She'd smashed a bottle and was holding it up to his face. This was getting serious. You could feel the whole bus stop not wanting the bus to come.

—Go. Do it ya fuckin maniac, he said.

She pressed. I swear, in the silence, I could hear the glass scratching against his skin. She clenched her teeth and her elbow went up till it was level with the bottle.

—Come on, he said.

But she couldn't do it. Instead she turned to us.

—He's a paedophile! she shouted across.

None of us reacted. She stepped onto the road, flung her arms out and explained.

—He likes wee lassies. He shagged my wee sister and tried to put her on the game.

He put his hand over her mouth and his other arm round her waist. She slipped out by dropping to her hunkers. Pushed the ragged edge into the paintwork and gouged a line that said I hate you all along the length of the Beamer. I expected him to go ballistic now. But he stood with what looked like calm on his face. It might have been resignation. I realised later it must've been calculated anger. The precursor to revenge. Once she got to the tail lights and the bottle slipped off smashing on the road she collapsed crying. He went over and helped her up.

—Come on, was all he said and guided her to the car.

When he drove away he stared at the line of people at the bus stop. It looked like he was asking our forgiveness. No, not that – our understanding. And hey who wouldn't understand? We'd all been in situations like that. The whole bus stop. And I think I can back that up because nobody tutted or criticised or said what's the world coming to. They sighed and were lost in a memory of when they were the entertainment. The Beamer stopped at the lights and he was still watching in his mirror so I waited till the lights changed before I left the bus stop. When I walked away so did twenty others.

The clouds had cleared and it was frosting up by the time I got to the Green. I ate my kebab on a glittering bench watching the prostitutes coming out for the night. Shivering. Their arms wrapped round themselves. The kebab was cold. The chips were limp. Dead chips. I threw them for the seagulls to catch mid-air. As they flapped about me like good ideas I thought about that script editor. I wondered if she was still beautiful. Because telly ravages people before their time. I was thinking how good it would be to meet her now. And tell her the story about how we love an argument. How we don't want it to be over at all. How there's a duality, a longing for it to stop vying with a need for it to go on. Like being on a rollercoaster. But the need for it to go on is stronger at bus stops in Bridgeton, Glasgow, Scotland. But she would just lean forward, put her hand under her chin, and say Really in a tone that sounds like interest but is just dismissal.

After the gulls had swooped all the chips I was walking past the prostitutes and realised how young they all were. Some could still be at school. Most were alright, a couple of ugly ones and three or four pure babes. In the right circumstances they might've been picked up as models or actresses or something. Hey – they might've been starring in a Soap. But here they were down on the Green freezing their arses off for whatever reason.

—Looking for business?

It was her. She'd changed into clean clothes and her face was a mask of lipstick and powder. But her eyes were overflowing with smack. She had a burst lip and a black eye she couldn't cover up with powder. But it was definitely her. The white sandals.

He Ain't Heavy

It's an old Victorian sandstone bridge with the BBC at one end and posh houses at the other. It must've looked good in its heyday but now it's lined with cars so you never see its full grandeur.

But I was walking slow with time to spare and summer coming in. A young woman brushed past as if the world was a needless impediment. Even her curves and the glossy backs of her thighs were hateful. Halfway across was sat this guy. He started singing at her.

♪ You're gorgeous.

She tracks a safe trail between him and the dusty line of parked cars. But his song followed telling her how gorgeous she was. The further she got the more his singing distorted to shouting. He stopped when she turned the corner but kept watching like she might come back.

I gave him a fright when I said, —Looks like she's not coming back.

He looked up and into my eyes before he spoke.

—They never come back, he said and took a slug of warm cider from a blue plastic bottle. And the way he said they never come back had a sort of burden in it. A something that made me think.

—She's BBC, he said when he'd drained the bottle. And

7

that explained it. He had a couple of recent cuts on his baldy head and his right fist was scabbed up.

—Fall out with a door?

—Brick wall, he said, bang! And he mimed punching a wall.

—Used to do that all the time, I said, showing him my scars. He checked and believed with a nod.

—I'm always fuckin doing that me, he said.

—You from Blackpool?

He was from Burnley. His eyes were blue. His clothes had been clean a couple of days ago. But even though it was getting hot, he didn't smell except for cider and nicotine. I told him how I used to live in Blackpool but he didn't want to know. He wanted off the subject and well out of Lancashire. Told me how he flits from Ireland to Scotland. Cork in winter, Inverness in summer.

—See this, this here bridge, it's a top of the pops spot this is. People going by all the time, okay toffs they are, but sometimes they drop me the brass like eh? And d'you know what the good bit is?

I didn't.

—I can see up their skirts.

I was still laughing when he said no that's not what it was.

—Cops cannot see me when they drive past. All cops can see is line of cars and bobbing heads of beautiful people on their way to BBC. That's how I got the cuts on head and the busted fist me. Cops came up in George Square asked me to move on. Gave them a barrow load of fucks I did, so they arrested me. I struggled and in drunken rage I laid into bottom of big statue.

—Aye, I said, —I'm like a Gremlin on the drink an all.

He burst out laughing. —Gremlin. Fuckin Gremlin, that's a good one, he said, —Fancy going for a sup?

8

—No. Can't. Been off it fifteen years, I said.

He held my gaze in them powerful blue eyes and said,
—Congratulations on your fifteenth birthday.

Well, him saying that: he knew what it meant and I knew what it meant. And he held his hand out and we shook. As he tightened his grip he cried. And as he cried he seemed to be slipping away from me. Down. I thought he was going to fall right through that bridge into the river fifty feet below.

Then he started singing.

♪ Happy birthday to you...

And he laughed.

And I laughed.

And he sang.

♪ Happy birthday to you...

And some posh folks went by but he sung as if I was the only person in the world. He wasn't being caustic. He was genuine. I stood there and took it. Like I deserved it. And looking at him I realised I deserved something. Whatever had happened, luck or chance or Divine Intervention – it could just as easy be me on that bridge as him. The twists and turns that brought us both here would be miniscule. Little decisions that led to little actions that gathered together to form a path. This was the day two paths crossed. And we spoke about that. In them terms. We didn't shirk from the spirituality of width nor the philosophy of depth. We mined that subject till we'd dug up truth. And by the end of it we were joined somewhere.

Then I told him about Paul, my brother, who's down and out an all. In another town. I told him a funny story about the day I went up a close and there he was, my brother with three other alkies. About how he gave me a hard time. And how hard it was for me with all the guilt and self-loathing cos

I wanted out of there, away from my brother.

—But you stayed.

—Aye I stayed, but I wanted out of there.

—But you stayed, he said. —You fuckin well stayed.

—He's my brother, I said.

He caught my eye and said this:

—That's right. He is your brother.

And he thumped his chest three times lightly. There was something holy about the way he done it. If people were passing I don't know. But I'll tell you this: something happened. My heart sprung open and there was an outpouring of compassion. Or the hindrances to my compassion broke away. Or the world's compassion flowed in. Or something.

Something.

He seen all that and he winked.

—Aye he said, and winked, —I'm the same. But I just can't break free.

—Listen, I said, reaching out to shake his hand, —Thanks.

—You know what I'm going to say now don't you?

I didn't. But I felt it would be profound.

—Few quid for a charge?

I gave him a fiver, laughing. He thanked me with a wink and a punch on the arse as I walked away. I was nearly at the other end of the bridge when he shouted.

—Hey!

I turned. He stretched his arms up and sang. His Opera Singer voice had everybody looking.

♪ He ain't heavy, He's my Brother.

I laughed, gave him a fist in the air and turned the corner. At first I thought he was talking about Paul. But then I realised exactly what he meant.

Jif Lemons

Our Danny never had much of a nose for danger. And that nearly got him killed. After years living on the breadline he went to Gamblers Anonymous. Within a month he'd saved up four hundred and bought a wee Proton. A couple of weeks later he got a full set of freshwater gear out the yellow paper. That was him set. Ten years ago, before his gambling took off big style, Danny was regular in the tranquil places of Scotland. The lochs and salmon rivers. There wasn't a bit of waterway in the country he didn't have a fisherman's opinion on.

All week at work he went on about how this was a new start. How there was nothing like turning off the engine into that hissing silence. Getting the rods on the water, building the fire and settling down to watch them floats. The picture he painted made a big impression on Timmy. He asked Danny if he could come. He was fed up with weekend Neds making life a pure fuckin misery. Danny wanted to be up in them Highlands alone. He wanted the first breaths of serenity in ten years to be his own. But he felt sorry for Timmy. Timmy was only thirty but being a natural worrier he looked fifty. And Neds always pick on the weak so they'd panned his windows so many times Timmy put council shutters up. Steel. All weekend they'd slam bottles and rocks off them. It was

11

probably shellshock he suffered from. If he phoned the cops
the Neds would stand there with their palms out. What? Us?
Rocks? Does somebody live in there? Soon as the cops left it
would be like the battle of the Somme. All Timmy wanted
was a weekend without fear. Danny put a big smile on and
told him no bother. Of course. The company would be good.
Somebody to talk to.

—Yes! said Timmy and punched the air.

So as they put the last touches to next week's work
schedule, Danny caught a glance over and for the first time in
years a flicker of delight crossed Timmy's face. He'd scribble
away worrying about the schedule then his head would tilt
up. A smile appeared. His eyes wrinkled. And Danny could see
the very mountains Timmy was dreaming about.

They left at half-four. Timmy brought the bright orange
waterproofs you get on building sites and a wee fishing
rod he'd got for his tenth birthday. Danny had a good hour
laughing at that rod. How these big fuckin salmon would
snap it in two first bite and eventually got Timmy to fling it
out the window at Killiecrankie.

—I'll give ye one of my rods to keep ya wanker, said
Danny. And off they went up the A9.

Timmy sat slack jawed at the scenery. That's when Danny
asked him if he's ever been up the Highlands before.

—Is Saltcoats in the Highlands?

Danny gave Timmy a wee slap on the back of the head.

—Saltcoats? Saltcoats? Ye mad?

Turns out Timmy'd never been anywhere without houses,
roads and shops. So as they turned off for Tummell he
marvelled.

—And not a Ned in sight, said Danny.

It was all backpackers and cars with kayaks and canoes.

People eating noodles by the side of the road. Some waving. Some simply looking in the car. But without menace.

They parked under the dropping branches of a tree so the car couldn't easily be seen. When they got to the head of the loch Timmy stood staring down that water while Danny set up the rods. Every now and then he'd hear Timmy saying wow! Or fuckin hell man! Two rods for Danny and one for Timmy. Timmy loved his new rod and kept asking if he really could keep it.

—It's yours. Scrape your name on it.

He showed Timmy how to tie the hook, set the float and cast. Then he got onto the floats. It never takes him long to get onto the floats. Danny claims to have invented them. Jif Lemons with a curtain hook screwed into the bottom. You put the line through the hook, slide the float to the required depth (Danny was expert at that an all), wrap the line round the top and screw the lid on. See them for miles. In white, grey or rough water you could see them. Once these three lemons were floating nicely out in the loch Danny lit the fire. They had a conversation about the smell of burning wood and cracked a bottle of Buckie each.

Life didn't get any better. Relaxation took ten years off Timmy. He leaned back on the grass and laughed. Looked up to the sky and shouted

—Sky.

—Sky.

Letting his voice raise up to the heavens.

—Sky.

—Sky.

—Sky.

—Your float just bobbed, said Danny, watching as Timmy ran down to the water's edge and grabbed his rod.

13

—What will I do now?

—Wait till it bobs down again.

Danny got beside him. Two men, four hands on the rod. Ready. Waiting for that fish to swallow the bait. They waited. But the float stayed where it was. And the water was calm. Danny's grasp slackened.

—Must've been a nibble just, said Danny, —Good sign but.

He left Timmy holding the rod by the side of the silver loch and the sun coming down to the mountains in the west.

An hour later as the water was turning red they heard a car. It parked behind theirs and Danny was relieved to see it wasn't fishermen. It was just a guy and his bird. They got out laughing and came over. Nice night and all this. She had great sticky-out tits and a short skirt more for clubbing than wilderness. Timmy blew some check-that-out air though his pouted lips. Danny offered the guy a charge of the Buckie.

—Cheers mate.

—Danny.

—Cheers Danny. I'm Tam.

—That's Timmy, said Danny.

—All right Timmy my man.

—This is Lydia, bird.

—Hi yi, said Lydia, and shook hands.

They could smell her perfume.

Tam produced a joint and they sat by the fire smoking. Danny was sure Tam caught Timmy checking Lydia's legs out. Caught him and smiled. Nudged her. Leaned in and, Danny said, told her to tug her skirt up that bit more. It was red knickers she had on. Right sexy red knickers. Tam kept asking about fishing and even though he didn't sound like a man interested in fishing Danny told him.

—See they floats?

—Aye.

—Know what they are?

Tam shrugged.

—Jif Lemons.

—Jif Lemons?

—Fuck aye! said Danny, proud of himself.

—They things ye use in cooking? asked Lydia.

Now he had them interested Danny described in detail how he invented them. How easy they are to see, no matter the weather. How fishermen all over the country use them now. The world even for all he knows. But do they give him the credit? No, do they fuck! All the time Tam's rubbing his hand slowly up and down Lydia's leg. Timmy and Danny catch each other's glance about that whenever they can.

Dark is falling and when Danny's on the difference between a salmon and trout's tail they hear another car. It parks behind Tam's and two guys in their early twenties get out. Tam waves over.

—They're here, says Tam to Lydia.

Over they come.

—Get it? says Tam.

—In the car, says the one that looks like a gypsy. The other one looks like a junkie. He stands saying nothing. Staring at Lydia's legs. Not even looking away when she catches him. Stares till she puts her head down in fact. They've got a carry out and toss a can each to Danny and Timmy without asking who they are. They sit down, the junkie close to Lydia so their legs are touching. Tam starts rubbing her leg again and the other guy rolls a joint. And all this is done in awkward silence. Danny and Timmy fiddle with fishing tackle and throw some more wood on the fire – the flames lighting them all up. Then Tam, in an artificially happy voice, points to the floats.

—Guess what they are?

—What?

—They yellow things.

—What yellow things?

—Out there.

The junkie looks. —Floats, he says.

—Aye but what are they made out of?

—Floaty stuff, says Gypsy and bursts out laughing, choking on smoke. Rolls over onto the grass and laughs far too much. Tam boots him.

—No – Jif fuckin Lemons. N'at right Danny?

—Aye, says Danny. But nerves are setting in.

—Tell these two bams how you invented them, says Tam.

Danny proceeds to tell. A burr of fear unmistakeable in his voice. By this time it's getting dark.

—That's great, says Gypsy when he's finished, —I'll have to remember to keep my Jif Lemons.

—Talking about lemons, says Tam, and gets up trailing Lydia by the hand to the cars.

He takes something from Gypsy's car and goes to his own, opens the back door and says something to Lydia. She crawls in backwards and lies on the seat. Everybody's watching as Tam takes one ankle and places it on the head rest. Her other on the parcel shelf. Danny and Timmy can't believe it.

—D'you want fucked ya slut, he's saying as he drops his jeans.

She says something.

—I can't hear ye, d'you want fucked?

There's a whimper that sounds like a yes.

—I can't fuckin hear ye, and he slaps her. She yelps.

—Yes! she shouts.

—Yes what? he says holding a fist in the air.

16

—I want fucked.

Bang! He punches her. She starts crying. In he goes and closes the door. Danny and Timmy stare out at the floats. But the two other guys don't take their eyes off the car. There's a slap and a yelp. Gypsy lights a joint and takes a long suck as if he's trying to quench his lust. The muffled cries of Tam shouting at Lydia and the rocking of the car are hard to ignore. Especially when nobody's mentioning it. When nobody's talking at all. When nobody's saying nothing.

Then comes back doing up his jeans with a grin and hands Gypsy the red knickers. He immediately stuffs them to his face drawing in air. Danny and Timmy are down at the waterside checking rods that don't need checked.

—What the fuck is this? Timmy says to Danny.

Danny shrugs.

—Does this happen a lot? Timmy asked.

Danny shook a quick no and tried not to look at these guys. When he did Tam was tranquil as you like smoking a jay; looking over the water. He caught Danny's eye and winked.

—Aye, is all he said.

—Fucksake Danny he's a psycho, whispered Timmy.

—They'll probably go away soon.

The other two were in the car now. Shouting obscenities at Lydia. Taking turns fucking her. She started screaming. At first just like she did with Tam but soon loud.

—No. Please no! she was screaming.

Timmy gave Danny a what-will-we-fuckin-do look. She screamed louder and Danny knew what punches sounded like. The heavy thud of flesh against flesh.

—No. Help. Help. Rape!

Danny automatically took a step but Tam put out a hand

—Leave it, was all he said. Danny turned back to Timmy.

   —Help, help. Rape!

   —Shut it ya wee fuckin hoor!

Another heavy punch. Lydia's face at the window pleading. They drag her back down. A heavy punch. A scream. Danny goes to move again.

   —I said leave it.

   —But.

   —Get back to your Lemon Jifs and mind your own business, Tam said.

And he meant it. Then he stood up and went to the car. Opened the door. All movement stopped. Tam lit a torch and ran it's beam all over her body. Molesting her with an obscene pool of light.

   —Hit her a slap, he said.

Somebody did.

   —Harder.

Somebody did.

   —No Tam please, she said.

Tam closed the door and the punching took on a new ferocity. Danny and Timmy moved closer. Danny could hear exactly what Tam was shouting.

   —What you doing in here with them ya wee slut?

   —They raped me Tam.

   —Raped ye? You're a slut. You took them in here.

   —I didn't Tam honest.

A punch.

   —I didn't Tam honest

A punch.

   —Tam please.

   —Right lads, he said like an order.

It was like drums the punching. She screamed.

—Fucksake Danny, said Timmy.

—Rape! Rape! she was screaming. Banging her fists on the window.

The torch sent a series of lurid silhouettes flashing at Danny and Timmy. Danny was sure her face, caught for a second in the berserk light, was covered in blood. He crept closer. Timmy behind him. Closer they got. Closer. They were all raping her. Her face was bruised and bloody. Punching her sporadically. It was only when they flung her so that her face smeared on the glass that she seen Danny. And she froze long enough for them to react. Tam jumped out.

—What did I tell you?

—What the fuck are yees doing to her?

—What did I tell ye? Tam said as he went to the boot.

—I can't stand here while youse rape somebody.

—What did I tell ye?

Danny tried to answer but couldn't.

—To mind your own business.

The boot's open and there's this almighty roar. A motorbike coming at them it sounds like.

But that's not what it is.

It's a chainsaw. Tam lifts it roaring from the boot. Danny's off bumping into Timmy as he does. He can hear the deafening roar of the chainsaw inches behind.

Danny sprints screaming into the darkness. Crashes into and over a fence. Lands on his back. Gets up and runs. Hears Tam clambering over the fence and in and out the trees. Between the revs he shouts.

—Come back here ya bastard I'm goanny cut ye up!

It's heavy going with them big chest waders on. But Danny keeps moving clump clump. Running through a puddle. But keeps going. He can hear Timmy screaming somewhere and

19

by the cadence knows he's running too. Danny struggles on. The puddle gets deeper dragging him back. The roar of the chainsaw and Tam's mad voice closing in. The more the water drags Danny back the more effort he puts into going forward. The chainsaw diminishes but he's not stopping. Not for nothing he's stopping. The water gets up to his knees. Up to his arse. Up to his chest. But he trudges on. One leg then the other leg. Then he loses his grip. Next thing he's swimming. With the high waders dragging him under. But he swims with the determination of terror. He swims for a long time. And even though it's early summer the water is freezing. It's a full half-hour before he feels rocks and gets some kind of purchase. And all the time the sporadic roar of the chainsaw and laughing and shouting.

The water falls to his chest, his arse, his knees. He gets out and does a kind of handstand to empty the waders. Gallons cascading out onto his head. The he starts running again. Clumping in the direction this big black shape. Maybe it's a house, maybe it's a house, maybe it's a house. But he's soon on this dark shape. Up he goes steeper and steeper until he's actually climbing. When he gets so far and so steep that he can't climb any more he stops. By now the chainsaw has stopped and he thinks he hears cars moving off. But he's not going back to check. He sits shivering. Praying for light.

And then there's Timmy.

And then there's Timmy.

—Oh fuck Timmy.

Danny starts crying. Timmy's first time outside town and this happens. He pictures Timmy's body parts floating beside the Jif Lemons. Danny dreads the coming of light.

Then

He thought he heard something. A sharp intake of breath.

A loose stone rattles down the slope. Danny grapples about for a rock. A weapon. Finds a hand-sized pebble. And if ever he was capable of murder, that was the night. He can feel somebody listening in the dreadful silence.

Then,

—Danny?

—Timmy!?

Timmy comes scraping down the slope and lands beside him.

—Thank fuck, says Timmy, —I thought you were dead.

—I thought we both were dead.

They hugged each other. Crying for who knows how long.

—Danny, said Timmy after a while.

—Aye?

—I don't want to go fishing again.

All their tension came out in laughter. But they had to stifle it so they giggled like schoolboys till the sun came up. And that's when Danny seen the puddle he'd run through. It was the loch. And across the other side the Neds' cars were gone.

—Thank fuck, said Danny.

—Danny? said Timmy.

—Aye?

—I can see the Jif Lemons from here.

And sure enough away in the distance were these three floats.

They made their way down the mountain. Crept round the edge of the dawn loch. A heron flew through the mist. And there was silence. When they emerged from the trees Timmy spotted the chainsaw drowned in the water.

—Don't touch it, Danny said, —Evidence.

Danny pulled the rods in one at a time. The Jif Lemons

tilted and headed in. Nothing on the hooks but nibbled, bleached worms. He packed everything away and made to the car.

He knew there was something different about it. Everywhere was little crystals of glass. Every window smashed. And something on the roof. Like a branch. No, not a branch. It was a gouge.

When they were right up close they realised what it was. The roof was split open like a tin of beans. The ceiling hung down inside like guts. There was a few gouges on the doors where they'd not been able to cut through. The seats were shredded and the insides had avalanched.

—We have to go to the cops, Danny said.

They shoved the gear in and started up. Bumped that wreck of a car along the dirt track. It was only when they got to the road and the wheels started ringing they realised the tyres had been shredded too. Danny screamed.

The drove into Kinloch Rannoch with sparks coming off the rims. It was pandemonium on wheels that drew up to the cop station. But there was nothing the cops could do. They needed the girl to make a formal complaint. The only good news was, that even though Danny was third party fire and theft the insurance office paid out. It was the best story they'd had in years, they said.

Now, at nights, way up the Highlands, far, far into the wilderness where nobody can come, Danny sits watching a lonesome Jif Lemon in the knowledge that guys like that could be anywhere.

I Thought You'd Give Me Pills

Floyd was dying. He was on a towel flung on the bed and his breathing was bad. Connie would be chirpy for a while then she'd burst into tears. I'd hold her and try to comfort her but it was no use. I was angry. It was a bad bit of my personality. It went like this – unpredictability would turn to anxiety, anxiety would turn into fear, fear would turn into anger, anger would turn into aggression, aggression would turn into violence, violence would subside and I'd be left with guilt and remorse.

She could sense I wasn't sincere so she pushed me away, went into the garden and cried. I smashed a few plates off the wall but that didn't make things any better. I felt useless. When she came in she just glared and went back up to the bedroom. I didn't know what to do and to tell you the truth I wished the cat would hurry up and die.

She'd had Floyd since long before we met. She'd a lot of memories tied up in that cat. Stuff that would never be easy to let go. I tried to think of solutions through my anger. Maybe there was something on the internet about FIV?

I found a page with this concoction of herbs and vitamins. I raced into town and got them. I expected him to be dead when I got back but he wasn't. He was lying on the bed sucking his ribs in and out. Every expansion and contraction looked painful. And Connie was sharing every pang.

I mixed the stuff and put it in a syringe. Floyd shook his head and let out a noise that said he didn't like it. He was a ginger tom who was always skinny but now his face was clapped in. He looked up at Connie and I swear he was saying for fucksakes put me out of my misery. He winced in pain as this concoction hit his gut.

—Oh my wee boy, said Connie and held tight as she could. But he didn't purr and he always purred when she touched him. I clapped him light on the head but my heart wasn't in it. I'm a coward. I wished I could go away in a tent for a few days and come back once he was gone. I tried to comfort Connie but my heart wasn't in that either. I was useless. Fuckin useless. I went into the garden. There was an electricity of anger all about me because the other cats and dogs wouldn't come near. And they wouldn't go up the stairs either. They sensed death.

There was a Krusty living next door at the time. I kinda avoided him because he was full of saving the planet by himself and mad esoteric ideas. He was special. If only you knew what he knew you'd be a better person. He was the last cunt I wanted to speak to.

—What's up?

—Alright Kenny, I said.

—Catching a blues vibe here.

He used to catch these right obvious vibes. The strain was all over my face and I was bent over like a comma.

—Cat's dying, I said.

—What's wrong?

I told him about FIV being the cat equivalent of HIV and how Floyd was like a son to Connie. She was in the room with him and I was hoping he'd die soon. Get it over with. Kenny gazed up at the room and closed his eyes gently. Tilted his head to the tree-shagging Gods.

—He's not dead, he said.

I wanted to fuckin punch him.

—I know he's not dead Kenny cos if he was fuckin dead Connie'd be screaming the house down.

—Stay cool man ye need a calm vibe when there's illness.

I was about to tell him to get to fuck when he tells me he's got this mate Zak. Not long moved up from London. He's into alternative medicine.

—How alternative?

—Radionics.

Kenny said what he does is takes a hair from the patient and puts it in this wee glass tube. He inserts that into a machine with knobs and dials all over it. It analyses the hair and then Zak decides on the treatment. Now, I had been reading an article about Chinese medicine on the net. It was something like what Kenny Krusty was on about. They took a hair and analysed it. Depending on the structures of proteins they got a picture of the fluctuations in your health over the time it took that hair to grow. My anger started to subside. Here was hope.

—Where does he live?

—Near Whithorn.

—He takes a hair and puts it in a machine?

—Aye.

—And analyses the hair?

—And then decides on what treatment he's going to give.

—Does he do animals?

—I could ask him.

—Go'n phone him Kenny. Eh?

When I burst into the bedroom and pulled a bunch of

hairs out of Floyd's arse Connie thought I was losing my mind. I told her quickly,

—Kenny Krusty's got this mate who's got a Chinese machine that analyses hair and tells what's up and prescribes medicine.

Her face lit up. Kenny was at the front door shouting up.

—Have to go.

I kissed Connie and left her with a smile on her face for the first time in days.

It was a semi derelict cottage. They'd done up a couple of rooms and it was an ongoing project. Zak was over six feet but gentle and slow moving. He thought about every sentence before he spoke but not in a way where you felt he was calculating. His wife was out-to-here pregnant and made the coffee. Kenny had to go, he was showing somebody how to conjure up their Spirit Guide.

He left me with Zak and his wife. He'd been a big shot in finance. Had a nervous breakdown and got out. Done the whole positive thinking mind body and spirit alternative medicine thing when he hit upon Radionics.

By the time he'd finished telling me this we'd walked the length of the cottage. Here was this room. Sure enough there was a machine with rows of knobs and dials and wee glass tubes. Some had human hair in them and were lit up. One lime green, one yellow and another one deep blue. It was kind of pretty. There was a state of the art computer. It was obvious the machine analysed the hair and the computer sorted out the data. It was a good set up. The machines looked like old Bakelite radios only instead of Stuttgart Oslo Paris Moscow and London there was these symbols I'd never seen before. Chinese probably. Zak sat without speaking, touching the dials now and then and clicking at his computer.

He nodded and 'mm hmm'd' like a doctor as I told him about Floyd. He took the clump of hair and loaded it into a glass tube. Put the tube in the machine and turned a knob. The tube glowed pink and lit Floyd's hair up. There was this buzzing and although it was coming from the machine I felt like it was coming from me too. I really thought this was going to work. Zak adjusted a dial and flicked his computer keys. His wife brung some coffee. We drank and chatted about everything except Floyd. There was a bleep and the pink light turned red. Zak leaned across and moved a few knobs and dials.

A long time after I'd finished the coffee I got the feeling he wanted me to go and he'd still not gave me any medicine. I was too shy to ask. Maybe he forgot about the pills? His wife said they had to go before the shops closed. I left thinking maybe it took a few hours to analyse the hairs and he'd phone to come and get the medicine later.

When I got home Connie was upbeat but worried. Floyd was getting worse and you could see he was in more pain. She looked at me eagerly as I told her what happened. I could tell she was waiting for pills.

—He never gave me any pills. I think the machine takes a while to analyse the data and then he'll phone us.

She sat with her head down, stroking Floyd.

—Will you sit with him till I go to the toilet?

I clapped him, feeling good that I'd been able to do something. Okay, I'd lost my temper that morning but here I was not being fuckin useless.

—Daddy's getting ye a magic cure, I said and he looked up at me. He opened his mouth to meow but couldn't. Instead of being red the whole inside of his mouth was white. I don't know where it came from because I'm not one for the crying.

27

But the tears cascaded out. I felt terrible for the wee fucker.
He'd had the bad luck of nine cats and here he was dying
in agony on a towel on top of the bed. Connie came back
in and cuddled me. I don't think she'd ever seen me crying
before. And something else, my tears meant more to her than
all my anger, all my running about looking for a cure. Our
relationship went deeper that day.

It was starting to get dark and still Zak hadn't phoned.

—Did ye give him our number?

I realised I didn't. And he forgot to ask for it.

—He could get it off Kenny Krusty easy enough.

But it was starting to bother me. And when Floyd sicked
up the latest batch of internet concoction I decided to
drive over. It was a surprised Zak who opened the door. I
could feel puzzlement as we walked to the room of dials.
Floyd's hair was still lit up red. We had a strange and uneasy
conversation. He asked how the cat was.

—He's getting worse.

—Worse? He seemed surprised and turned the knob a bit.

—Ye can tell he's in pain every breath, I said. —Connie's
breaking her heart.

He leaned in and inspected the dial.

—She's had that cat since he was a kitten, I said. —Lost half
his skin once when he fell into a hot bath. Went missing when
he was weeks old and lived in the roughest part of Glasgow.
Kids tormenting him. When he came back he was wild.

I don't know why I was telling him Floyd's life story. I
suppose my thinking was the more he knew the easier he
could make up the medicine. He listened and said something
that surprised me.

—He should be improving, I've been treating him for four
hours.

—Eh?

—I've been treating him for four hours. Since you came here earlier.

I didn't know what to say. He tapped the big Bakelite machine with the middle knuckle of his index finger. Did he give me the pills? Nope I'd've remembered that. I was focused on pills. I was fuckin obsessive with pills. Nope – he never gave me no pills.

—When will it be finished analysing the hair? I asked.

—Pardon?

I pointed at the little part of Floyd bathed in a red glow in its glass house. The buzz seemed louder.

—The hair? Does it usually take this long to analyse?

He looked at me a bit then said, —Ah! It's not that kind of machine.

He went on to explain what Radionics was. The whole universe is made up of different vibrations. Using Floyd's hair, the machine picked up his particular vibrations. It analysed these for anomalies. Once it found them a specific coloured light came on. That was the machine sending new vibrations through the cosmos to Floyd. These new vibrations would kick him into the correct frequency. That's when I noticed the machine wasn't connected to the computer. My face was falling and he could see it. He knew I needed more.

Right, he said, and got out a wee board that said yes on one side and no on the other. There was an arch of numbers from one to nine and some of the same crazy symbols that were on the knobs and dials machine. He opened a small wooden box and took out a pointed crystal on a chain. He was pulling out all the stops. I didn't say anything. What could I say? He started the pendulum swinging away and back. Away and back.

29

—Is Floyd going to be well? He asked.

The pendulum to yes.

—Is Floyd going to be with us for a while?

The pendulum to yes.

—How long is Floyd going to with us?

The pendulum drifted to four.

—Is that four weeks?

The pendulum stayed back and fro.

—Four months?

It stayed where it was.

—Four years?

The pendulum swung with force over to yes. He turned to me.

—The crystal is never wrong. The crystal says Floyd will be with you for four years. Nothing to worry about. Just go home and let things take their course.

He stood up indicating softly but firmly for me to leave. When I said it, I said it like a wee boy,

—I thought you'd give me pills.

I remember exactly what he done. He held his bottom lip with his thumb and middle finger. He looked at me and looked at the machine. Then he spoke.

—Do you want pills? He was totally sincere when he said that.

—I thought you'd give me pills.

—I can give you some pills.

He opened a drawer. There were hundreds of small bottles. All the exact same. And in these bottles were hundreds of white pills the size of pinheads. All the exact same. He scattered some on a sheet of dark card.

He lifted the pendulum again and swung it over the pills. It was making me dizzy to watch.

—Just getting them up to the right frequency, he said.

Something made me want to laugh. But I didn't. He gave me the pills and adjusted the knob.

—To account for the pills, he said.

I nodded. I fuckin nodded!

Connie could see the disappointment. But when I told her all about it we laughed. We did laugh. Despite everything we thought it was funny. And we decided we'd be as well using the pills. You never know.

Floyd struggled on for three days and Connie stood vigil by his side. Not a wink of sleep did she get. I admired her all the more for that. I seen something stronger in her than me. On the third day, at four in the morning, he was in so much pain we phoned the vet. She knew why we were coming and got out her bed to meet us. She'd said not to leave it too late. Not to let him suffer. It's sometimes hard to let things go but, as Connie said later, life is falling off a cliff sometimes.

It was horrible and I never want to see it again. Floyd curled in pain on Connie's lap on the way up. He let out a noise that made me and Connie burst with a cry of real despair.

—Aw fuck, look at him, I said.

She leaned over, her hair hanging round him like a curtain.

—Floyd son, Floyd – it's mummy!

He died.

I'd stopped the car. We sat at the side of the road in the early morning light and cried.

—Poor Floyd. Poor fuckin Floyd, I kept saying.

—There my wee darling. You're alright, Connie was saying. —You're alright now.

We looked at each other. There was no hiding the tears

this time. I leaned across and hugged her.

The vet confirmed he was dead. She never said anything but we knew she thought we'd let him go too far. And we did. We put him through pain he shouldn't have went through. On the way home I started ranting about Zak and his Radionics.

—If it wasn't for that cunt we'd've made the decision earlier. Put Floyd to sleep.

But Connie could see through that one.

—Don't blame that big guy. He was only trying to help. He never even charged us any money. If it wasn't Radionics it would've been something else. It was us. It was our fault.

She was right. We'd learned a lesson. Don't let your love hurt. The pain we didn't want to feel was passed onto Floyd. We buried him in the garden under the rhododendron bush. We got a beautiful statue of a forest baby cheap in a garden centre and put it down as a gravestone. It's got a peaceful smile on its face. Sometimes I sit there and remember the nights I used to lie on the couch with Floyd purring on my chest. It makes me smile.

Nine-Eleven

It's funny, no matter how we try to dress it up, events are always personal. The first thing I thought of was Tony.

It was six in the morning when we climbed the Rest And Be Thankful. The engine was struggling. The jukeboxes, pool tables and fruit machines in the back weren't helping. I peered over and was glad we weren't going fast enough to lose control. Away down in the valley was a white cottage. It looked like a toy. Somebody came out with a dog and from this distance they were hardly moving at all. We passed the Jesus Died for Our Sins rock that takes you off that precipice onto a high moor. Both of us sighed at the same time.

—Praise the Lord, said the apprentice.

—I hate that bit an all, I said.

I was glad they'd sent Tony with me. He was only nineteen but he was six feet something and built like a Wurlitzer. I was only thirty so we were more like pals really.

That day we replaced fruit machines, pool tables and juke boxes all along the Kintyre peninsula. Every barmaid or barman asked if we wanted a pint. And we always did.

Tarbert. Fix one machine swap the other. One pint each. Clachan. Fix the fruit machine. One pint. Ballochroy. Jukebox out of order. Change fruit machine. Two pints each. Bellochantuy. Swap jukebox. Sort fruit machine. One pint and two malts each. Kilchenzie. Install pool table. One pint each. Drumlemble. Replace jukebox. Miserable bastard. Carradale. Rock guitarist playing Hendrix crashed guitar through slate. Change slate. Three pints each.

By Machrihanish Air Base we were drunk. Americans love mechanical slot machines. They had two rows of Bell Fruits. We repaired the faulty ones and tested the rest. Went along setting jackpots and checking the money came out smoothly into the trays. I left the coins for the guy behind the bar. They were no use to us, quarters. When we got to the van there was the usual three cases of this American beer called Budweiser. They called it Bud. And two hot American pizzas. In we got.

—Will I pull the pin on a couple of these General, Tony said.

—Yes siree, I said.

We drank them on the drive to Machrihanish beach. Got ourselves the best two seats in that powdery sand. These things were real pizzas. Not deep fried or the painted-on-dough things we got then. We scoffed them looking out to sea. Washed them down with Bud. Talked about America. Tony had this auntie in New York. He'd been there twice and she was on the lookout for a job for him. She'd just found one with prospects. And he was going over at the end of summer.

—I've got you a job with the Fire Service Tony, he said, impersonating her, —Your uncle Patrick's seeing about a green card.

Tony was good at it. It was a Scottish accent with a tinge of America. Sounded like somebody trying to put it on. Or somebody that had it forced on them.

—More prospects than that dead end job you've got,

34

she said, —Dragging pool tables and jukeboxes up narrow staircases, she said, —A bad back by the time you're twenty-five, she said, —What kind of life is that? she said, —You can go all the way to the top in America, she said, —There's nothing to hold you back in this country, she said.

—What kind of life was slugging, what do they call them again, Buds and chewing giant American pizzas in the sand dunes? I said. —Driving along Machrihanish beach, I said, —With the wide Atlantic booming in, I said, —Next stop America out there in the big blue yonder. D'you want to leave all this? I said.

—The waves waving way way away in the U. S. of A., he said.

—Here tomorrow gone today. My pal Tony's flew away.

—We've took that to poetry again, Tony said.

Every now and then we'd take it to poetry. Mostly when we were drunk out our tits. But this was the kind of place that made you poetical. And to tell you the truth, with the sun turning the sea blue-green and this flock of birds flying tight to the water and that electric tang in the breeze, I couldn't understand why Tony wanted to go to America.

—And maybe never come back? I asked him. —Are you alright with that?

But he just shrugged and asked what was there here? Except the sea corroding the rocks and the reek of rotting seaweed? And Glasgow? A fuckin slum, that's what Glasgow is. You could see what he meant. At that time, '80 or '81 it was, Scotland was on its way down. But Tony was young and he had a dream.

His auntie in New York was right about one thing. My back was done in already. It wasn't going to last much longer. I felt that my life was over. If I couldn't humph slots what

could I do? That's all I'd ever done. And it was good to get
the free drink. Where was I going to get the free drink? Tony
was staring ahead but he wasn't seeing Scotland now. He was
seeing America. I could see the stars 'n stripes in his eyes. I
was going to miss the big cunt. He loved being on the Kintyre
run with me. The other men didn't drink so he'd be sober.
And bored. He said I was wild. Mental. Never met anybody
that could drink like me and still stand up.

Well that day we paddled a bit, kicking water over each
other and laughing. We were still laughing when we got
back in the van. It was me that started the song but he soon
joined in.

♪ Oh say have you seen by the dawn's early light, we sang,
as we drove south towards the Mull of Kintyre.

Tony went on about how the job we were doing was cos
of the Americans. Rowe Ami juke boxes, Wurlitzer, Seeburg,
and the pool tables. We were delivering bits of America to
tiny fishing villages and hamlets. These villages, he said, were
lusting West over that ocean. Water falling from the rocks
like saliva – drooling for America. I had to admit he had a
point. We were all part American now. There was no getting
by that.

♪ Oh Campbeltown loch I wish ye were whisky –
Campbeltown loch och aye! Oh Campbeltown loch I wish ye
were whisky, We would drink ye dry me and him och aye aye
aye aye aye. That's what we sang every time we seen the sign.
Campbeltown.

A few jobs there then that was us finished. We usually
ended up in the Argyll with Archie. Give him a few bags
of fruit machine tokens and he'd fill us a bottle each with
whisky and lemonade.

—That'll keep yees going on the way down the road lads,

he'd always say, then launch into his amazing stories about brawls with Yanks. The more Archie battered the Yanks the more they came to his bar. Archie said he was giving them the genuine Scottish experience. They liked to fight. And by a stroke of luck, so did he. He was the highlight of our trip, Archie. Not to mention his lovely daughters. I'd liked Marie for years but never been able to pluck up the courage. My heart was beating for Marie but nobody knew.

We took a big breath, put our best smiles on and crashed in singing.

♪ Oh say have you seen, by the dawn's early light…

But it was quiet and empty. Just two old guys in the corner. Not a Yank in sight. No Archie either. His wife was behind the bar and Marie was serving. I thought he must be in jail again.

—Where's Archie?

The two old men looked up and went back to their conversation. To their pipes.

—Archie passed away, his wife said matter of fact like. —Two weeks ago.

Marie hung her head and watched us through her hair. His wife gave us a whisky each and told us how the drink finally got him. Liver. Died in Lochgilphead. His wife and all his daughters at his bedside. The whole Air Base turned out for his funeral. They even done a fly past.

That day we praised Archie to his wife and Marie and anybody else that would listen. It was all stories about Archie. Stories that for the living are scandalous but for the dead are legendary. There was a time that night when it was only me and Marie at a table.

—Marie… I said.

But she put her hand on my arm and looked in my eyes.

Then she got up and walked away.

It was a pretty sombre journey back towards Glasgow. We drank a few cans of Bud. Tony couldn't believe Archie was dead. He'd been throwing lefts and rights just last month. Re-enacting his latest battle.

Tony fell asleep at Bellochantuy. In his sleep he was making this noise that sounded like crying. By the time we made Lochgilphead he was snoring and I couldn't get Archie out of my mind. He was in my head laughing and throwing punches one minute then I had to swerve to miss him. He was in the middle of the road shadow boxing. When I braked there was nobody. Nothing. It was three in the morning and the commotion never woke Tony. Only moved him forward so that his hand fell into the empty Bud cans piled up to his knees.

I rolled the window down to stay awake and crashed open another Bud. A few miles south of Lochgilphead I seen lights behind me. It was the cops. I flung the can into the verge, stopped and got out, trying to breathe away from him. But he was right there looking at Tony slumped forwards.

—He's sleeping, I said.

And he could see the pile of pizza boxes and cans on the floor.

—He's drunk, I said.

—What's in the van?

—Fruit machines and jukeboxes. Pool tables.

He wanted a wee look. My speech was a wee bit slurred. Especially saying jukeboxes. Shook boches. He looked at what was in there and got the vehicle check back over his radio.

—That's fine, he said, —I just stopped to tell you one of your tail lights is out.

I promised to have it fixed back in Glasgow. As I got into

the cab he said this to me,

—Watch yourself. There's a few drunk drivers about up here.

There wasn't another soul on the road. I said thanks and he knew what I meant by that. And off we went. It would soon be dawn. The tail light wouldn't matter. I think I nodded off a couple of times on the road to Inveraray. I was determined to keep my wits about me for the Rest And Be Thankful. So I drove with my head out the window for ten seconds, in the window for ten. My face was coated with dew. My skin

Was
Coated
With
Soft
Dew

I jerked awake at the Jesus Died For Our Sins rock. But it was too late. Sparks flew from the side of the van as we toppled over the barrier. Tony woke upside down with his back pressed to the windscreen. A look of surprise. I could feel the fruit machines and jukeboxes floating in the back. And we fell.

And it was just all them New York firemen going into them two buildings. That's what brought it all back. And the weight of guilt floating about inside me like the fruit machines and jukeboxes. So that every time I crash. I crash hard.

Big Brother

Despise me if you like but why should I be up for eviction this week? I've put a lot more into this house than Cassio. But they've nominated me. Me and that so called artist. I can see why she's got to go, big mouth, no talent. Reminds me of this joke: this girl about thirty, massive ego, no talent, goes into a bar with a parrot on her shoulder. The barman says: Where did you get that? And the parrot says: Up the Film School there's hundreds of them up there.

But this Cassio guy, he's only fit for hanging about the girls. If he's not in his bed pretending to have a buckled knee he's in the Jacuzzi. Drinking wine. Killing me with his Scouse accent. I can see right though him. He might be into kick boxing and body building but in a fight I'd rather have my wrinkled Grandmother beside me.

And the other Housemates adore him too. Especially Othello. That thick lipped darkie prancing about like a Nancy boy. He's done this and that, been in more fights than Tyson; so he says. The girls are all over him. Take that Irish bint Emilia, for instance. All over me like a cheap suit the first week. Had her wrapped round my little finger. Could have had her wrapped her round my body too. And maybe I did? There are some spots the cameras can't see.

I had a word with Othello. Stay back. But he pushed his

chest out and leapt into my seat. Plumped down between
Emilia and Desdemona on the couch. That was the night
we got *Shakespeare in Love* as a reward for the fitness task.
As his black skin changed colour in the flicker of the screen
I hatched my plan. I was going to be here at the end. The
hundred grand would be mine. But winning's not enough.
Othello and Cassio would have to lose. And lose big. The
further into the movie we got the more I grinned and the
more I grinned the better my plan plotted out. And the more
it plotted out the more powerful I felt. My oh my. It's good to
be bad.

I've studied human psychology. Read all the books.
There's only one lesson worth learning: watching people. I've
devoted my life to watching people. Observing. I've learned
what hurts them. The face is the cinema of the soul. When
I was working for the Brennans I had to collect unpaid drug
money. I tugged nails. Tongues. Eyelids. Genitalia. Used
electricity. But physical pain's the poor cousin of emotional
pain. I've ground people down with that. Broken hearts.
Turned them into puppets. I learned the emotion that
destroys men quickest and most completely. The green eyed
monster. Jealousy. That's where my plan was heading. Down
into the deep green sea.

After our week three circus tricks task we had a few
bottles of wine and Emilia was playing her guitar. It's hard to
imagine being patronising by guitar playing but she managed
it. She sang 'Morning Has Broken' like she was singing the
true wisdom of the world down to us. After that, Desdemona
sweet whispered Othello into a massage, lying there with her
bra off and her breasts flattened into the cushions.

I moved into action. Firstly, I took Cassio aside and told
him how I was certain he was going to win. How I had seen

it in a dream – no – a vision. Everybody loves to be praised. But to be praised and tempted with a hundred grand; that's a heady Macbeth mix. People are so gullible. I kept slipping vodka into his red wine till he was pissed. We sang some manly songs and I brought up Desdemona. By this time Othello was giving her reflexology. All she had on was a skimpy pair of black panties.

—She's pretty fit the Desdemona eh? I said. As Cassio laughed his glazed eye was on that love heart shape a woman's ass makes where it disappears between her thighs.

—She is a bit of a babe, says Cassio.

—Would you? Eh? Would you?

—Yeah she's a fit bit of skirt like mate, says the Scouse prick. And who hears him but Monty and pulls him up.

—Less of that talk in here, Monty says. Cassio asks who he thinks he's talking to and presto, the place erupts. Drink and men's one thing but add women and it's magnesium in a glass of Andrews Liver Salts.

They cut the cameras and sent security in. Put us to bed. Said they'd be watching. First light of dawn I heard Othello ask Cassio what happened. Cassio was sobering up and you know how psychologically weak you are then. I intervened.

—It was Monty, I whispered and led Othello out into the kitchen. Cassio thanked me with a wink before pulling the duvet over his head. In the kitchen I told Othello everything. How Cassio is lusting after Desdemona. Othello laughed the cavernous laugh of ignited jealousy and said he wasn't worried about Cassio. Solid as a rock him and Desdemona. I upped the stakes.

—But what would happen if you get evicted and Cassio stays?

And left him with that.

Next morning in the Jacuzzi Othello's ignoring Cassio. Cassio asked me what was eating him. I said it was his lager lout behaviour last night.

—Maybe I should apologise, he said.

—Good idea. I think you should, I said. And as he walked away I stopped him. —Idea mate, I said. —Take it or leave it?

—Go on.

I suggested maybe he'd be better making his apologies through Desdemona. He seen the sense in that. Oh my! Things were warming up nicely.

That night Cassio cornered Desdemona at the chickens.

—Oh look at those two Othello, I said to his bulbous eyes. Don't they look like two lovers making up after a quarrel? If we didn't know you and her were, you know. Isn't that just what it looks like?

He dismissed it with a weak smile.

Desdemona promised to mend things. Straight into the kitchen she went and did the girlie thing with Othello. Flicking her hair about, standing close, that sort of thing. He bent and he broke and he promised to talk. Soon as the opportunity arose. I am a camera.

The sun went down and I sent Cassio to have another word with Desdemona. In the Jacuzzi. Then I steered Othello out – and divine intervention – Cassio was sliding out the Jacuzzi like he'd seen Othello approaching and was climbing out of guilt.

—Something doesn't look right, I said.

Othello stares him out and Cassio slinks away. Of course Desdemona's not too pleased at the atmosphere. She comes up cold in the summer breeze.

—He's only worried that you're ignoring him, Desdemona says to Othello. And off she goes to salve Cassio. I spotted a gap in Othello's rage.

—When you initially fancied Desdemona, I said, —Did Cassio know about it?

—Know? Ha! It was him that let slip to Desdemona on my behalf!

—Is that right, is all I said. And the silence I left hovering over the bubbling cauldron was enough. I waited. It was only the sound of the pressured air bursting the surface.

—Okay, say what you mean and mean what you say, goes Othello.

—I'm not going to blacken someone's name on a slight suspicion.

—What slight suspicion?

—Don't go there Othello – it's not a good place to be.

By now we were watching Desdemona and Cassio through the glass.

—Look! Desdemona likes to party. Where's the proof in that?

—It's just the way she acts when Cassio's about.

The churning water was sweet discord. If music be the food of love then chaos is the food of hate. Play on.

—You do know she lied about her background to get in here? She told them she used to be a nun when she attended a school run by nuns. She's out for herself. For fame. She's using you.

—Using me?

I nodded and as he considered that I whipped up another whirlpool.

—Do you want to look like a wanker on national TV? There's sixteen million people watching.

I had him. I bloody well had him.

—You need proof that something's going on between

them, otherwise the public'll think you're a nutter.

He looked at a camera.

—Put off the talk with Cassio and just watch what happens. Study. Examine. Let her prove her innocence to you.

From that moment Othello went downhill. Tossed and turned in his sleep. Abrupt with everyone. He was sure to be nominated soon. He'd sway this way and that. Desdemona's innocent – oops there she goes sneaking off to the unseen corner with Cassio. And all the time Cassio was watching Othello. Cassio craved reconciliation. He couldn't live in conflict. The look was one thing but Othello read it as another. I was balancing him. But I pushed the fulcrum too far and I woke up with his hands on my throat. Foaming at the mouth he was and demanding proof of Desdemona's affair.

—The strawberry boxer shorts, I squeaked. —The strawberry boxer shorts!

Cassio was asleep. Othello sat back.

—They're mine, said Othello. —I gave her them.

—Cassio was wearing them yesterday, I told him. Othello crept over and peered under Cassio's duvet. His boxers were black. Shining like sex. He came back.

—If this is true I'll give him such a kicking. And then, then, I'll sort her out. The slapper.

I waited till Othello was sleeping. I had to be quick cos he only slept an hour at a time. Woke up in jealous rages. I snuck into the girls' room and stole the strawberry boxers. I stuffed them to the bottom of my suitcase. Next day, after lunch, everybody was lying in the garden sunbathing. I told Othello this was the time.

—What time?

—Ask for the boxer shorts!

He asked Desdemona for a pair of boxers cos his were all in the wash.

—It's hot – don't wear any, she said, and winked.

—I want to.

I followed them to the girls' room. Listened at the door. She throws him a pair of black ones.

—No – these will be too small, says Othello.

As she searched for another pair Othello made like he suddenly remembered the strawberry ones.

—What about them strawberry ones I gave you?

She looks at him and sighs. She searches. And she searches. But she can't find them.

—That's a bad omen, says Othello. —The first gift I gave you and it's lost.

Othello starts rummaging through her bags. Then she gets an idea. More divine intervention. She accuses Othello of displacement activity. An obsession to put off the reconciliation with Cassio. And to ice the cake she starts going on about how great a guy Cassio is. How he could learn a few things from Cassio. A diamond geezer.

—It's nothing to do with boxer shorts is it?

—What are you talking about?

I hid as they came out. He follows her to the boys' room where she finds six pairs of clean boxers under Othello's bed. Holds a pair up between her thumb and forefinger.

—Wear them and grow up, she says and storms off to the kitchen.

Othello burst out of the room.

—What's wrong? I said.

—Everything!

Othello went off in a huff. So I caught up with Desdemona willing the kettle to boil with folded arms.

—What's wrong with him? I said.

—I think he's jealous, says Desdemona. —Of Cassio.

—Of Cassio?

—Cassio, she said flinging her palms out.

—Has something happened that I don't know about? I asked her.

—Not that I know of.

—His mind's not right. I said and walked away leaving her bewildered in the kitchen.

That night Othello snuck out of bed and into the girls room. I walked on all fours behind him like an animal. When he leant over her bed I was beneath it in the darkness. In the mirror I could see his face changing from hatred to love to betrayal. My, it was a glory to watch. A sheer glory. Then what does he do but lean forward and kiss her.

—I'm nominating you out this week darling. And he kisses her again. —I can't have you in here with another man while I'm here.

Desdemona wakes up and his tear's halfway through the darkness. It drops onto her bottom lip.

—What is it Othello?

—We're finished – it's over, I'm nominating you for eviction, he says.

—Othello! she whispers, but he walks away.

The next day all is dark and silent in the house. Cassio comes up to Othello and asks him something. I can't hear but they go into the boys' room. I can't follow them. Too obvious. Next thing the girls are summoned. Then everybody, one at a time, except me.

Then Cassio calls a meeting round the dinner table. They were all waiting for me. I can't believe I trusted you and all this they're going. Othello is affronted that he put so much

48

trust in me and this is how I repaid him. I kept denying it. But thump, up on the table goes my suitcase. Othello produces the strawberry boxers.

—What have you got to say about that Iago? goes Cassio in his Scouse accent.

—At the end of the day, you live by the sword. You die by the sword. That's all I said.

Jock Tamson's Bus

From up here Glasgow could be a South American city. I half expect a condor to go soaring over the plateau. Clouds moving over the streets are casting lochs of light on estates and schemes without prejudice. The Red Road flats are bleached monuments then plunged into darkness.

Out west Ben Lomond pokes its snowy head. East, the two blue gas tanks in Lanarkshire button the city's grassy scarf to its rock-hard body. Like a man's man – Glasgow is a city's city. It's New York – without the guns. Or it used to be – before the guns came.

The bus bends round Castlemilk Drive and there's a faded old sign on the side.

GLASGOW CITY OF DESIGN AND ARCHITECTURE

And I'm thinking we're all architects in our own wee way. Anything we don't like we change. We redesign people, places and things. That's where architecture and design begins; in our minds.

The driver's behind his people-proof Perspex. He believes we're all out to get him. Or his bosses believe it. Or the designer of the bus. He stares downhill, both hands gripping the wheel, all knuckles and gold sovereign rings. The hairs on his arms vibrate so you can't tell if it's him or the bus that's purring.

—St Enoch's mate – much is that?

—Pound, he says, without turning. He won't turn. He might see something he doesn't like.

I ting the coins down the chute. They sit in their own little prison – glass walls both sides – so that I can see the driver can see he's not being cheated. He releases one hand and click – there's a whirr and a ticket hangs out the hole. I've been accepted. Baptised with paper. The paper's floating up and down on the breeze. Happy to be free. It almost squeals when I rip it off. I walk into eyes. No words. I'm scrutinised – even the wore-down heels of my boots burn. An old man's hands hang over the seat in a holy triangle. The trinity of ordinary life. It's a church the bus. I march up the aisle and plant myself in a pew. I could pray breath-coloured prayers onto chromium handles. But people are watching. Listening with their eyes.

Everybody stops looking at me when the bus lurches downhill towards the city. I check out who's who. What's what. The man in front of the woman in front of me turns and talks to her. Not in a bus voice – when your words are private but their volume is public. His words are a murmur. And his tight black hair is amazing as light runs over his bowed head. And dark. And light.

There's a Young Team behind me – quiet and bent over in a we're-rolling-a-joint pose. Advertising their machismo. Behind the Young Team there's two Spice Girls giving it listen-to-me-bus-talk.

—So I just turned right round and said Oh d'you think so? And she went Aye – so I goes – try it then and she comes – I'm feart I catch something. So I gets her like this and then Smith came in – Right Girls – keep your lovemaking for after school he goes…

—He never.

—He did.

—No!

—Honest to God!

—Smith?

—Aye!

—You should report him.

—For what?

—A teacher's not allowed to say that.

As she talks she's taking up positions. Engineering her body through a dictionary of attitudes. A thesaurus of moods. A mime artist of incredible subtlety. Expressions a Director would die for. She doesn't know the name of the play she's in. Maybe it's act one of the farce of the rest of her life. Maybe it's a comedy. Or a tragedy. We'll never know till the end. And the audience are repulsed and entertained. Oprah. We could kick ourselves for listening – but we listen – and we never kick ourselves. Never. We're created so that we can't kick ourselves. Our morality is always for other people – other places.

Her face has settled to a sneer the girl. Now what would her architecture be? Her way of looking at the world? New. All new. Red and yellow plastic: iPod-tastic, probably. Sneering at anything that stinks of the past. And she's got a point – it's called Castlemilk. Her and her pink pal get conspiratorial – huddling together. Giggling through each other's hair till they can't speak at all. A raised hand – an open mouth – the delightful fall into laughter. Must be sex. Most people on the bus smile – if not with their mouths with their eyes. Then we scan elsewhere for entertainment.

The man in front of the woman in front of me's scratching his face. That's the first I see his scar. From his temple to his chin. At least twenty stitches and black scabbed blood. The woman laughs and dunts him gentle on the shoulder.

—See you! she says.

His eyes smile and his face tries to follow. But the scar's too sore so he presses his palm on the scar and smiles. A half smile. Laughing out the side of his mouth. He probably lives four up in a close. All pish and shite at the bottom. And maybe some needles. And blood. Aye that's it – blood on the close floor. Eight closed doors – two on every landing – you can never tell what's going on behind them. Never take a door for granted.

The bus drones into Croftfoot. The low down four-in-a-block flats with gardens sneer up the hill. All private. Better cars chat by the kerb-side. Leaning back from the bus in disdain. Further along – semi-detached houses sneer at the four in a blocks. Bigger cars snuggle up in driveways. All I Want Is A Gravel Driveway, strikes me as a good Country Western song. Or maybe it's Punk Rock.

We're a right worrying crew. The Spicers are passing the joint back to the Young Team. A flock of baseball caps glide on a cloud of smoke. Theirs is the anti-tecture of up closes – burns – grass parks – corners. Knives and now guns. Now guns. And walks designed to shock. The swagger that brands you. The stare perfected to drive home fear. Neds and Nedesses flirting with what they fear most. Violence. One's hung his legs out to dry over the chair beside me. Ninety pound trainers with a hundred pound stink.

What gets on at Croftfoot is different coats and perfumes. Teacher and Doctor walks. Where the shoulders go forwards and backwards instead of side to side. People are taller. Skin is tighter. And life is oh so mellow.

The Croftfoot folk separate into an impossible mathematics of seats. Einstein couldn't work out how they all got seats without sitting next to one of us. The Neds and Spices stare. But Croftfoot doesn't look back. The bus is a tense orange oblong roaming the great streets.

By Hampden everybody's noticed the scar. Catching a glance when they can. The Spices nudging each other and making secret faces. For Croftfoot; their mother's Glasgow's come back. Slums and razor gangs. They said it was gone. The new cosmopolitanism had wiped that out. But the man with the scar's still talking low and tickling the wane. And putting his palm to his face for smiles. We slow down. And down.

And down.

The man stands. Everybody watches out the sides of their eyes. Or through a lace of eyelashes. The Neds talk louder about guns and chibs and swords. His big hands grapple with seat after seat. Leaving a finger shaped film of Glasgow manhood. And little rainbows when sunlight catches them. He's swimming his way to the door. His shoulders built for another time – digging – or lifting – or constructing ships. Demolition. The bus nudges. Hisses. The doors open. Pressure is released.

Hampden glints like pride. The man with the scar suddenly comes charging back along. Everybody's not looking. His shadow passes over one relieved person then the next. He reaches the woman.

—Sorry hen, he goes and kisses his wife. Kisses the wane. —See ye at six my wee darling – chookity choo, he tickles her and she laughs.

His architecture crumbles and rebuilds. Maybe he's not in a pishy close. Maybe it's one of them new houses up Castlemilk. The ones people who left years ago are buying back into. The ones shaped like ships. The wife smiles.

—See ye the night Joe. We're having fajitas.

Joe does his palm to face stuff. The wane smiles. I smile. Joe smiles at me. The bus smiles. Everybody. Off he pops Joe. What a guy! We love him. Joe's great. The whole bus loves him.

And we're amazed at half a smile in window by passing window. The other half of his face sleeping in a palm of pain. Frame after frame our minds are changing. People even looking at each other and shaking their heads. Admitting it. For a minute Croftfoot and Castlemilk don't exist. We're all on Jock Tamson's bus.

As we leave Joe behind we're rearranging our thoughts. As we pass over into the city, in the distance you can see the sun glinting off the new buildings right along the river. Glasgow reaches for the sky. For all we know it could be a Brave New World.

The Blue Hen

In Greenend me and John up the stairs shared a garden. It
was the early eighties. Everything was grey. The pavements.
People's faces. The buildings. The sky. The future. Nobody
had a job. Not one solitary single soul. Men were gathering
in bigger and bigger numbers on the corner – passing Buckie
and dope. Unemployed moulders and turners and puddlers
tugging away at joints. It was one big party. But smack was
coming onto the scene. Bannan worked beside me and John in
The Klondike. A moneylender. He took to dealing like a duck.

Things started to change. John noticed it before me. I
goes up for him this night – I had a bottle up my jook. I was
anticipating the first slug burning its way down my gullet and
hitting my belly like a mother's love.

I chaps his door and he peeks out the letter box. I push the
Buckie bottle up till the golden cork's poking out my jumper.
But John wasn't going down the corner that night. Or the
next night – or any other night.

—The corner's stepped over the line, he said. —There's no
way back now.

I could see what he was saying. Needles were on the
corner. And last week Bannan stabbed a welder from
the Whifflet trying to move in on his patch. He's in the
Monklands; critical.

If John's not happy with the corner, I'm not happy with

57

the corner. So we sat in his scullery drinking. John says there's
corners all over the country like it. Men gathered up. And it's
a holocaust, only it's not bodies that's piled up and destroyed
but souls. People's spirit.

—By the turn of the century the whole country'll pay for
it. Mark my words, he said.

It was making him angry so I asked what about the
garden, what's our plans? He looked out over the garden.
Thinking. Then he turns and says,

—Things're tight and they're not going to get any better.
If ye want to at least keep your dignity you've got to have
goals, long term plans.

John thought we should get chickens. It was a great idea.
I took a swig and handed him the bottle by way of a toast.
We figured we could get six or even a dozen eggs a day. That,
with the carrots and radishes and spuds we were already
growing, could save us a fortune. Soft boiled eggs and
omelettes were lighting up in my head.

Next day we went round the Whifflet library and
researched on chickens and eggs and hutches. The hutch
was easy enough to build, we got the wood from the swing-
park fence. Bannan's maw was looking out her back window
wondering what the sawing was and – hey! – off walks an
eight feet section of council fence. We never thought we
were doing any damage cos the swing-park had no swings,
just some broken slabs and a universe of smashed glass
shrapnel. Sometimes on a clear night if you stared into the
particles starlight would be in them. You never knew if you
were looking at the ground or the sky.

A week later and four eight feet lengths of fencing, we've
built a chicken run. In the book it says to hang a hundred
watt bulb inside so the chicks can huddle round it. I ran the

wire from my house cos I had my Powercard meter wired up
to run for nothing anyway. John took the bulb out his back
room that they never used except if they got visitors and
I've never seen any of them the three years I've lived in the
bottom flat. All we needed now was the chicks.

We went down to Bankhead farm where they were doing
chicks for fifty pence each. Twenty we bought, a tenner, and
that was a lot of money to us. We put them in and watched
the wee yellow cartoon characters buzz about searching and
pecking and sniffing in their new home. But they're not as
daft as they look, chicks, soon they were all piling over each
other to get below the hundred watt bulb. The cheeping and
the smell of sawdust and all them chicks squeezing into the
light made me feel good. A wee yellow ball of life. Me and
John smiled at each other. It was a great feeling and we both
looked forward to omelettes and soft boiled eggs. I know
that because we talked about it all the time.

At night I'd sit at the window looking at the slither of
warm light beaming across the garden. I'd imagine the quiet
burble of the chicks pressing round the bulb. Snoring maybe,
if that's what they do. And then, now and then, one of
them falls out the bundle and scutters round the other side
and launches itself into the pile looking for a place nearer
to the heat of the great bulb sun god. The spuds and the
other stuff were doing fine in the garden. We'd even took
up some radishes and made pieces on margarine with a bit
of salt. The way they crunch when your teeth arrive through
the soft bread, mm! Well, the chicks soon passed that wee
lovely stage and turned into these pre-historic monsters. Their
crazed gaze said they'd tear the eye out your head if you
gave them half the chance. Sometimes, if John wasn't there,
and they were all staring at me I'd get a bit scared and have

to shut the lid. But if he was there I'd not mention it and try to see if I could see it in his eyes. You can't mention fear in Greenend.

On and on it went and they got bigger and uglier. Then one morning in winter I went out and there was one lying dead. I chipped a few stones up at John's and out he came with his maw's slippers squeezed onto his feet and her housecoat wrapped round him. We held it up by the claw and looked at the white slither of death over the ball of its eye. We were really worried that it could be some chicken disease and we'd lose the whole lot.

In the library there wasn't much about chicken diseases. It was mostly all good news about chickens, how to get the best eggs and stuff. We convinced ourselves it was natural causes and erased one soft boiled egg each from the future menu in our heads.

But when we got home and lifted the lid there was another one dead. Eye pecked out. Bloodied stalks hanging out the socket like fibre optics. So that's it. Fights. These chicks were now teenagers. When we looked about to see who was responsible every eye was evil, every eye intense. Like when I got my video knocked; every guy grinning on the corner the next day, I thought it was him. It's not easy to spot evil.

We talk about separating them into two groups and see what group's got a dead one the next day. But John makes an intelligent point,

—What if they're all killers!? And there's no getting by that, if they're all killers we'd need to put them in solitary confinement and I don't think the Burgh fence could take another hit. We went to bed that night a bit subdued but took the curse off it with a bottle of Buckfast between us.

Although John hardly ever got out his bed before twelve I wasn't surprised to meet him in the close at half-nine the next morning. He'd been up all night same as me, worrying.

We opened the lid together. Looked. Two dead. The rest chattering on the corner like Bannan and his mob. John shakes his head and leaves me to close the lid. He walks to the other end of the garden and kicks this old shed. He puts a hole right through it in fact. But that's nothing cos it's all rotted away. Just like this whole place; disintegrating. And he never says much, John, but when he does it makes a difference.

—Men don't lay eggs!

—What? I goes.

—Men don't lay eggs, he says with his palms firing out the meaning. I get it. I go and have a boot at the old shed myself. He's right, we got all them chicks but we never checked to see what ones were hens. For all we know it's all cockerels we've got.

What to do? The book wasn't much help. We looked for dicks and stuff between their big rubbery claws. But there was nothing to see. Then John came up with a great idea. His best yet. He's a bit of a psychologist is John.

—What applies to human beings applies just as well to chickens, he says. —The ones that've already died are probably male. All this territorial shite that goes on down the corner. Like Bannan and his drug-dealing. The cockerels are probably killing each other for control of the hens. It's a sex thing. Great! he says.

And I give him a how's-that-great look so he explains it to me.

—Well, how many of the corner team d'you know that attack lassies?

61

—None!

—Exactly, so if we let things take their course we'll be left with one male and the rest'll be hens!

That makes a lot of sense. For the first time in ages the whole thing takes on a happy glow. And something else John says too, the male that's left, that'll be the Bannan of the chicken run. If we start a breeding program we'll have the best genes in the pool. Christ! Things were getting better by the minute. Half of me wanted the weak chickens to be dead already.

By the end of January the happiness of that day had faded. There was only one chicken left. And it was a big Rhode Island Red. Male. Me and John couldn't believe how unlucky we'd been, we'd bought twenty chickens and they'd all been male. The very last omelette went pop in both our heads at the same time.

Then it started cock a doodle doo-ing at four in the morning. There was nothing you could do. People were starting to make comments. Not bad stuff, just:

—Is that your chicken I heard this morning?

Stuff like that. I discussed it with John but he seemed to have washed his hands of the situation. I knew he'd finally let go when the bulb went on the blink. Even though my electricity was stole, it was still me that was providing it for the chicken hutch. I felt it was morally right that John should provide the bulb. When I asked him he never said no. He just said that his maw had asked where the bulb was in the visitors' bedroom and he'd to go and nick one out the Doctor's. I looked at him. He looked back. There was no bulb coming out of him so I used the one out my toilet although I felt a bit resentful at the whole thing by now. And it's hard to shake off a resentment when you're getting woke up at four every morning by a big red rooster.

I decided not to fall out with John. So we chewed the fat as if the chickens had never happened. And we carried on drinking in his scullery cos by now the corner was a no go area and the red rooster ruled the garden.

That's why I was surprised when my door goes at half nine this morning. It's John and he's got the *Advertiser*.

—Wait till ye see this, he goes.

And he lays it out on the floor. We crouch down and he points to a wee advert. Blue Hen – three pounds. Apply Headrigg Farm Plains. I took in a big happy breath! John was back on the breeding program. And we had the top dog male out there ready to go to town. And! And this is important; and! – we know this one's going to be a hen!

Plains is six miles from Greenend. Six there and six back. I chipped in two quid and John chipped in a quid he stole out his maw's purse. And just to show me he was serious he brung a bulb down. He hands me it.

—Spare! is all he says. I put it in my toilet and he waited in the close. We had to act fast. There's no telling that a Blue Hen won't get snapped up.

It was freezing. One of them days when your shoulders rub off your ears. Our words were muffled by the fog they came out in. On the corner everything was arranged around Bannan. Like he's the hub of a wheel. Power, that's what it was. A few of the boys looked over. Some nodded but Bannan was staring us out.

—Don't look, says John, —Keep walking. Bannan shouted a few things but we kept going.

Once we cleared the corner I felt at ease. And so did John cos his head came back up out of his jacket. We strode out towards Plains. The snowflakes were coming down now and then like miniature saw-blades. They were cutting into our skin. But that's nothing. With a wee bit of imagination you can think yourself back into The Klondike at the furnace. Me and John and big Bannan having a laugh and a couple of cans. And the snow biting your face becomes furnace heat. That cheered me up and I imagined a year from now; hutches all over the garden and me and John out with trays collecting eggs. Selling them round Greenend. All these boiled eggs and omelettes rushed back into my head. I glanced at John and his thoughts were the same. We smiled. I mind the exact moment John smiled, a wee snowflake landed on the end of his nose and he licked it off. Going cross eyed at the same time. And we laughed. And he put his arm round me and gave me a wee hug. And I gave him one back. It was the happiest time of my life. We smiled on through the thickening snow. Two lights in the darkness of March.

When we got to Plains we paid three quid to a thirteen-year-old laddie. We told him all about our bad luck and our new breeding plans. He gave us a couple of tips and wished us all the best. The walk down the road was a lot quicker. The snow had took the sting out the air and we kept swapping the Blue Hen. I'd have her up my jumper for a mile then John'd have her up his. Chances each at being pregnant with the future. The whole world was that warm hen. I love the way snow effects sound. It was like beyond me and John and the Blue Hen nothing existed. The place was white and our footprints behind were driving us into the promise of uncharted lands of snow.

We were back at the corner in no time. Bannan was strutting about giving orders.

—Cross over, John said.

We crossed over. But Bannan seen us.

—Hey what's that you've got! he shouts.

—Ignore him, John says. We marched faster. Bannan kept on shouting.

—Stop! he shouts. We kept going. Out the side of my eye I could see him struggling in his jacket for something. Some of the corner boys were scattering. Others grinned with black holes for mouths.

—Stop!!

Bannan had a gun.

—John he's got a gun! But John pressed the Blue Hen into his belly.

—Keep going, he said.

—This is your last chance! shouts Bannan. That was the moment I seen what dignity was. It was John. It was the Blue Hen up his jook. The palms of his hands pressing her soft feathers. Dignity was John keeping on walking with that gun pointing.

The shot rang out exact same time as this groove made its way under the snow. A line like a pipe appeared between me and John. A pipe of snow bursting open at the seam. And a starburst of slush exploded at the kerb. I could feel the corner boys walking away from Bannan. I turned a bit as we walked. John never even broke his stride. Bannan pointed the gun again.

—John! I'm telling ye! Fuckin stop! he shouted. We turned the corner as the shot went off.

When we walked into the back garden John was shaking. That's when I realised so was I. We never said nothing about the gun. It was like it never happened. The red rooster swung its head round but it stood well back. By this time it was pretty adept at getting up onto the roof and that's where it went. There wasn't another bird up there. We put the Blue Hen in the hutch and watched. But the red rooster stayed on the roof. Out waited us. Watching. Glaring. We decided it was as shy as we'd be if somebody brought us home a woman to marry. It might be bold and tough but, as John pointed out, it's still a virgin and that's why it's bashful. Probably be alright in the morning.

I woke up the next morning about eight with this racket. A squawking like I've never heard. I ran out the back and there's John and he's just pulled the head off the red rooster.

—Murdering bastard! Murdering bastard! He's shouting. The claws of the red rooster are still twitching but the blood's spurting out its neck. Onto John's hands. Dripping into the snow. I look in the hutch and there's the Blue Hen lying stiff and dead beneath the ghostly daylight glow of the hundred watt bulb. Both her eyes are pecked out.

Bunch Of Cunts

This is just a funny wee story. There's nothing to it really but it cheers me up. We're up the West End Park this day. Me, Big James and Bonzo. We're smoking dope at the bowling green. There's nobody there. It's raining. Hissing. Bubbling up on the grass. But we're under shelter. We're not saying anything. Just enjoying the stone, the friendship and the silence. The air's cold and it's great drawing cool smoke into the lungs.

Next thing there's this hammering coming from up above. It's a big white *Gone With The Wind* wooden house. We give each other the I always thought that place was empty look and sneak up onto the green balcony.

Bonzo goes in. Me and James peek through the crack in the boarded-up window. There's a guy about fifty. A joiner. He's doing the place up. Bonzo chaps the room door. Three polite knocks. He's got his bunnit in his hands. Bonzo always wore a bunnit. The guy looks up.

—Mick in? Bonzo goes. The guy's puzzled. He looks about like Mick might be hiding in a cupboard. Or under the floorboards.

—Eh – I don't know. I'm just doing a Sunday in here.

—He says to meet him here at twelve, Bonzo says, as if his life depended on it. The guy stands up and his hammer's hanging down at his side. You can see he feels sorry for Bonzo.

—If he turns up I'll tell him ye were here, eh... He's

waiting on Bonzo's name.

—Jeremiah, Bonzo says. —Tell him it was Jeremiah.

Me and James are pishing ourselves.

—Jeremiah for fucksakes, says James, doubled over.

Bonzo comes out flicking his bunnit on and holding in his grin. His lips are white holding that grin in. We all tumble downstairs through the rain back to the bowling green. We smoke another joint and carry on as before. Silence. Smoking. Passing the joint. And the water on the sodden green is like a million dancing fairies. And the hammering continues in bursts up above.

After a while we're bored. We go up onto the landing again and do the same thing. Only this time James goes in. He's that big and glaykit James. Like a six foot Oliver Twist. The guy's up quicker and more suspicious this time. He's looking at James then past him to the open door. Trying to figure out what it's all about. But he can't see us.

—Is Mick there?

—Mick?

—Told me to meet him here.

—Who is this Mick?

But he's good James.

—Works for the council, says James, —I've to meet him here at one.

The joiner lights a fag and stares at James; trying to suss him out.

—Mick?

—Mick. Aye. That's his name.

—Who is this Mick cunt anyway? he goes, —What does he do for the council?

—He says I've to meet him here, is all James can say.

—Aye but who is he?

—He says I've to meet him here.

The joiner stares at James long and hard but James keeps his face straight. The joiner picks up a bit of wood and James can see the name Jeremiah written in pencil.

—What's your name?

—Ebenezer.

—Ebenezer?

James conjures up enough resentment to make him back down. He licks his pencil.

—Spell that!

The joiner writes it on the bit of wood then holds it up to James, pointing at Jeremiah.

—There was another guy up an hour ago. Jeremiah?

—Never heard of him, says James and you can see his face cracking.

—Wee guy. Had a bunnit, in his hands like this.

As he holds this imaginary bunnit, James shakes his head.

—If Mick comes in can ye tell him I was here? says James.

—Ebenezer?

—Aye.

—You don't look like an Ebenezer.

—That's what everybody says.

They stare at each other for a bit. Then the joiner says,

—Ok I'll tell him. And under his breath as James comes out,

—If I ever fuckin meet him.

We soft shoe it back to positions. The rain's not as bad now. We light another joint. We laugh but not outside. It's just really three grins out there across the flatness of the bowling green. Leprechauns we're like.

So after another while it's my turn. Up we go. I goes in. The joiner turns and sighs like I'm his millionth interruption. I go for the light and bouncy approach.

—Is Mick in? I says. I'm smiling but he's not.

—You're the umpteenth cunt in here the day looking for Mick.

—Is he not in then?

—Who the fuck is this Mick?

—Hey man. Cool the jets, I say, —Meets him in the Pop Inn Friday night, says if I wanted a start meet him here Sunday, two o clock. I want the job, so here I am.

—Well there's been guys in and out here all day looking for him. I think it's some cunt ripping the pish out yees all.

He looks at me for a while.

—What ye looking at me like that for, I says.

—What does he look like?

—Who?

—This Mick cunt!

I describe Bonzo to a tee. The bunnit the whole bit. That confuses the joiner all the more. He sits down puzzled. I know he wants me to leave.

—D'you not want my name?

—Name? I've had enough of fuckin names the day.

—But how will ye tell Mick I was here?

He stands up and gets the bit of wood. Licks the pencil and squints at me.

—Abraham.

—Abraham?

—Abraham!

—Your name's Abraham?

—That was my da's name, I says as if he'd hurted my feelings.

He writes Abraham on the wood and spins it clatter into the corner. Gets back to his work without looking at me. I creep out, laughter hissing through my teeth.

We're smoking on the green again. There's been no hammering for ages. You can just feel the joiner thinking it all out. He knows there's something but can't figure it out.

And he's still trying to figure it out when the three of us burst in, taking up stances like three guys in a musical.

♪ I will rock my soul, in the bosom of Abraham. We sings.

—Ya bunch of cunts, he says shaking his head. —Ya bunch of fuckin cunts.

And we all laugh. Me, James, Bonzo and that joiner. All sat on that floor on that wet Sunday afternoon, laughing at something we created, out of nothing.

Darwin The Wise Old Space Elephant

Call me Darwin. I am the Elephant that never forgets. However, I am no longer recognisable as an Elephant. I am merely a consciousness in the universe. Moving with many others; shoals of souls we are. I'm like a fish in the oceans of old, flipping this way and that in the blue light of the moon. Being pulled by the tides. But other currents move me too. I am driven by the tiny fluctuations of the cosmos. Attracted by the distant lure of stars.

Today, for reasons that will become clear, I have to tell you my story.

Long long ago all was peace on Elephant Island. All was calm. All manner of Elephants wandered. Woolly Elephants. White Elephants. Grey Elephants. Big ears. Small ears. Long trunks. Short trunks. Curly tails. Rudder tails. Sand feet. Webbed feet and on and on.

The Woollybacks basked in the silver water. Their long hair floating on the surface. Undulating. Whitebacks gathered by the river reflecting the sun. Sometimes, when I was young, I'd imagine them as great marble sculptures. Like the ones I'd sometimes come across half buried in the sand. Left behind by the forms that came before us on Earth.

Through the Whitebacks wandered the small Shorttrunks chewing away on bush berries a plenty. And towering above them the elegant Longtrunks sucked silver apples from the boughs of trees. When they tugged the branch would spring upwards flicking canary birds into instant flight. Lemon flapping on blue. Beyond them the Sandfeet padded the shoreline sending sound waves deep under the sand and out to sea. They loved the white frills of waves washing over their feet. Tickling. Now and then they'd throw up a trumpet of delight that would be answered by the Webbedfeet swimming through the clear ocean. Their massive legs trundling; aerating the sea for following fish. A time of peace and plenty it was. Contentment and calm. And because Elephants never forget we knew how we had arrived at that place. Our history.

Over the millennia we had adapted to our environment as it Changed and Changed. And Changed again. In the long ages of ice all of our species died off except for the Woollybacks. They carried our form through the narrow gorge of development. Then we would breed out again into magical variety. In the long hot desert stretches of time the Whitebacks would carry us until the heat died down. When there were only high trees the Longtrunks were our saviours. I am my ancestors. I am a direct link. Soul attached to soul attached to soul and so on and so backwards.

When I lived on Elephant Island, sometimes at night I would stand by the ocean thinking. Sometimes I'd just stand. The Webbedfeet would be swimming out in the bay. The waves would come and come and come. And never stop. I contemplated. I meditated. I saw that waves, though they came and came, each was different. Each was Change.

Sometimes, at night, I'd paddle out to my favourite rock and sit and think. Or just sit. I'd lower my trunk inches above the sea and suck the air of other places. The same urge that drove me to that rock drew my eyes to the horizon. The urge to be moving on. To be moving up.

On calm nights the sea would be smattered with stars. Little lights of hope out to infinity. Sometimes a brave, or foolish, Webbedfeet would trundle beyond where anyphant had ever gone. They would return speaking of two fears. The fear of the unknown fathoms of water, suddenly cold and deep, and the unknowable distance of the stars. To our knowledge nophant had ever crossed that sea. And Elephants never forget.

One night Great Brobotobo came carried in the cradle of three Elephants' trunks. Brobotobo's body had withered as his soul had grown. He knew the memories of all times. Even the forms before the Elephants. He could read the language of the sand. Hear the words of the wind and answer the whispers of the sea.

Brobotobo called to me perched on my rock and sent the others away. I waded ashore and once he checked there was nophant about, nophant listening, he spoke:

—Darwin. The time has come for me to leave, he said.
—To go... elsewhere.

Why was he telling me this? Of all the Elephants? He had seen me on my rock many times. Or standing at the shoreline. He had noted me as a contemplative, meditative individual. He told a story which I believe saved our race. I can tell you the story exactly, because an Elephant never forgets.

—There was a race once on this Earth. Intelligent and adaptive beyond measure. They rapidly adapted the environments they found themselves in. Colonised Pole to Pole and round the globe. On the sea. Under the sea. On mountains and in valleys. Along rivers and over plains. But then something strange happened. They adapted their environment fully to them. They adapted to it so efficiently they no longer needed to adapt themselves. When you adapt the environment to your needs you stop adapting.

Then the form stops adapting. Then after a time the form's mind stops adapting and when the mind stops adapting, the soul diminishes. The condition was known as Closed Mind. But they called it Utopia.

Behind Brobotobo I could see Elephants coming and going in the tropical forest. Happy and content. Brobotobo continued:

—When this race settled into their Utopia they lived in peace and harmony for a very long time. There had been war and strife but it became a thing of the past. There were some enlightened ones who tried to persuade the race to unharness the environment and let it freely Change. It was more insight than true knowledge. These enlightened ones were only paid trunk service. In the great cities trees were planted, grass was laid out, parks were planned. Here and there in little pockets the environment was made to look like it had been set free. But it was not the case. Peace and serenity cracked and this is why: there was one thing they hadn't considered when they constructed Utopia. They had believed that Form, which comes into this Universe as a gift, adapts to its environment because it is forced to. So when they had tamed the Earth they believed they had reached the end of their journey. Their final destiny. But the Divine Power is Change. Otherwise there is only stagnation. The force that drives us through the journey will not countenance stagnation. The journey is the meaning not the destination. There are no destinations, only pauses. Hiatuses. There is only Change and the growth of consciousness. We are all asleep; one day we will wake. Eventually disaster struck for this race. The force that requires Change amassed and accumulated until the dam of ignorance could no longer hold. Discontentment unfolded. Wars flared up. Hurricanes. Pestilence and flood. Famine and disease. These wars were different from any in their past. They no longer had the justification of religion or nationalism. They couldn't understand this force. They called it Apocalypse. The truth was simpler. If this Form would not evolve the Divine Power would compel it too. Form has to move forward. Expanding consciousness is the only goal.

I remember Brobotobo coming to the end of this tale. He turned to me and said,

—One thing would have saved them Darwin. Do you know what that is?

We stared out over the glassy surface of the sea. Sometimes stars would come and go in the sudden ripples of fish. Now and then a fish would tilt itself in the moonlight. Moonlight fish are my favourite fish. We thought for a long time, Brobotobo and I. We meditated. Contemplated. Golden dolphins meandered in and out of our thoughts. Eventually, when I was lost in the lap of the waves, Brobotobo spoke. He said,

—You're looking the right way and the wrong way.

He turned me to look to the shore and the Elephants going about their day.

—Look! he said. And he turned me to the water.

—Look! he said. Then the distant horizon.

—Look! he said. It made me feel uneasy.

—When the time comes – you will know what to do, he said. He kissed the thick of my trunk and called for his carriers three.

I meditated all that night. And the next night. And the

next night. And for many nights after that. The months passed. The years. And I moved from generation to generation, my consciousness growing always. That night with Brobotobo moved deep into my memory. But an Elephant never forgets.

One night I was on my rock when foreboding came. I remembered what Brobotobo had said about looking the right way and the wrong way. I took my eyes from the distant horizon and turned to the Elephants.

Just then a Whiteback bumped into a Woollyback. They sneered at each other in the darkness and moved on. Nophant apologised. Small though it was, that had never happened before.

All through the night I meditated and contemplated; insight growing in me. I mulled it over for many days and many nights.

One night a rainbow fish jumped from the sea, dazzled in the moonlight and sank back into the water. I thought of that fish. For a second it had hovered in absolute beauty in the light of moon. Time, thought and apparent reality stopped and I abruptly understood the universe in a bright one-pointedness. I was the universe and it was me. We were all the universe and all were me. Everything was one thing.

Plip! The moonlight fish dipped back into the sea and was gone. My heart beat faster and I turned on my rock. Worn smooth by the turning of many generations of me. I looked towards the river realising things had started to deteriorate.

And the next night as I contemplated, a Webbedfeet swam up and asked if I wanted a ride along the shore. Their feet had got so large and webbed they could carry huge weights and swim about easily and I must say at great speed. As we were travelling round the island I suddenly shouted:

—If you adapt your environment to you – you'll stop adapting!!

I tried to explain. He didn't understand. But Elephants never forget. I knew what I had to do. I gathered twelve trusty Elephants. Seven Webbedfeet, one Woollyback, a Whiteskin, a Shorttrunk, Longtrunk and a Sandfeet. We got on the backs of the Webbedfeet. One Webbedfeet led and we swam away from the shoreline. Leaving that land forever.

We found island after island after island. Populated large tracts of land and sea. Elephants never forget, every time we approached the stage of having adapted our environment to us, we let the environment Change and so Changed us; discovering ourselves. And when the environment could no longer Change, we moved on.

And moved on.

We kept evolving over time immeasurable to Elephants. Now, here we are; unravelled. Conscious but formless in the Universe. Shoals of souls we are. Free to roam. But we're still moving on and we're still moving up.

Today I am on the edge of the known Universe. Looking into where the Universe is moving out. The Cosmos is always changing. Always expanding. I turn back and the Elephants are going about their business. And their business is to be at one with the Divine Power. And two Elephants collide and frizz through each other. Almost taking form again. They pause in each other's fields for a moment then move on without comment.

Tomorrow we are moving on. I have picked twelve Elephant companions. We go to seek out our Maker.

Echo

Although my son Joe lives in a rough area he's never really been a Ned. He's more your Goth or Mosher or whatever them kids in black call themselves. White make-up and mangled music. Skateboards and scooters. I suppose he lives in a different town from the one I live in. When I walk along the main street I see backstabbers and danger. He sees potential new birds and computer geek pals. Maybe that's what they mean by parallel universes?

I remember what it was – we were going to buy Bruce Springsteen's *Greatest Hits*. I was trying to turn Joe on to The Boss. He never knew me the first ten years of his life and I was always making up for that. He was nineteen at the time Joe, big and gangly but despite being a Goth he was open to any kind of music. I'd already got him into Leonard Cohen and I thought he'd appreciate The Boss. I seen Jimmy the Hoover in the distance and nudged Joe.

—See him Joe – he was the best shoplifter in the town. Jimmy the Hoover's his name.

It was no exaggeration. Jimmy the Hoover had been banned out every shop of note by the time he was eleven. When he was twelve the Callons would drive him all over Scotland to do his thing. They had him on fifty-fifty. He was famous for it.

—He'd walk in Joe, I said, and shoom! Hoover stuff up his sleeves. Watches, Sony Walkmans, toasters, kettles, videos, tellys and couches.

Joe laughed. As far as I knew Jimmy was two years sober in Alcoholics Anonymous – a changed man. I shouted him over.

—Jimmy!

That's when I seen he was steaming. He was two steps forward, another one forward for good luck and one to the side. Any side. A carrier bag in each hand pulling his arms down like anchors. The bus swerved up onto the kerb to miss Jimmy as he staggered across to me and Joe. The bags swung out and hit me on the legs before his Buckfast breath enshrouded us. I realised I could've got away cos he was only beginning to recognise me.

—Aww! All right big fullah, he says so the whole main street turns round.

—I heard you were off the drink Jimmy? At the meetings?

He gave me a face between apology and defeat. Offered me a can of super. But I was still off it. Fourteen years all in. But I didn't want to rub it in or put Jimmy down. He offered one to Joe. Joe just screwed his face up politely. I was trying to make some quick small talk and get away.

—They're doing Bruce Springsteen's *Greatest Hits* at five ninety nine in Woolies, I said.

♪ Born down in a dead man's town, sang Jimmy. Loud.
—First kick I took is when I hit the grou – ound. End up like a dog that's been beat too much...

My body was leaning away in case he got to the chorus. But he stopped abruptly cos he'd finally worked out who I was.

—Stevie!! he shouted. —Your Paul's up the Chinkee's close.

I looked at him with a big what? on my face.

—Paul and his bird. This is our cargo. They're up the Chinkee's close.

Shit! If I don't go up and see him Jimmy'll say – seen your Stevie and his son on the main street. Paul'll ask if he told me he was there. Jimmy'll say aye and I'll be all the cunts. Anything can happen up closes. Then I thought – Ach! For all it'll be anyhow? A minute or two chewing the fat with my young brother. How hard could that be?

Up we go through the reverberation of our own footsteps. The light and the sounds of the main street fading. Paul's bird's a beached whale with dyed blonde hair. Kerry-Anne's her name. She's sitting on the wall and I swear the wall was bending underneath her. She's not right the lassie. She was pregnant for two and a half years once. Told the family she was two months and as time went by she kept on saying she was overdue, the doctor said it would definitely be in the next week.

—Anytime now Alice, she'd say to my maw. It was hard to tell if she was pregnant or not so at first nobody was suspicious. But once she was twelve months we started to click. After that my maw and sisters just humoured her. Is that right hen? Aw that's a sin. Can they not do anything for ye? Bring ye on? Something like that?

—I've to go in next week Alice, she'd say. —They're going to seduce me. But nobody laughed. It was a liberty to laugh at her.

—Look who's here! Jimmy says and Paul turns at an impossible angle. A can of super swinging between his thumb and middle finger,

—Paul look who it is! Look who it is! Kerry-Anne's shouting.

—For what hic do we owe the honour! Paul says. —For what do we owe the honour! Hic.

He came and flung his arms round me. By this time Joe was pressed against the wall, watching. He'd slipped into a parallel universe without noticing. This one.

—Must be a special occasion. That's all I can say – must be a special occasion, Kerry-Anne's shouting as Paul cries all over me.

Sobbing so much I could feel his chest pounding off mine and his back going up and down like a boned balloon. And d'you know what was going through my head? Not his tears. cos you can never trust the tears of a drunk. The only thing they're sincere about is where their next drink's coming from. What was going through my head was, I hope he doesn't spill that beer on me. If he does I'll stink of alcohol. I'll have to walk along the main street. People'll smell it and think I'm back on the drink. In this town it'll only be a matter of hours before my maw hears about it and starts worrying about me all over again. But then I thought – he's an alcoholic, he's not going to spill a drop. He's got the can in a mechanically sound pivot between his thumb and middle finger. The beer stays parallel to gravity as the can goes every which way. So I let him cuddle me safe in the knowledge he'd not spill a drop. In the background Kerry-Anne was still shouting. I couldn't really hear at first cos Paul was shouting.

—Shut it you. This is my brother come to visit me. Keep your mouth shut!

But she keeps on going and that's when I hear what she's saying.

—I want a cuddle, Kerry-Anne sobs. —I want a cuddle.

At first I think she's taking the piss but when Paul breaks off to slap her in the face I see she's not. She's deadly serious.

She does want a cuddle.

—What did I tell ye? says Paul and slaps her. The slap echoes round the place. Its ring diminishing as her pain increases.

—Fucksake Paul, says Jimmy and pulls him back.

Paul punches Jimmy full force on the chest. Jimmy reels onto his arse looking up at me. And I know, and Jimmy knows, and Paul knows the only reason Paul's not getting a doing is because I'm there.

Kerry-Anne stops crying.

—I only wanted a cuddle. I was only asking him for a cuddle.

Paul lifts his hand again and I grab it. He was never very strong and I was full of muscle. So I pulled him gently back and went over to Kerry-Anne. I got down on the wall beside her. My hands couldn't even meet behind her. She grabbed me and locked her fingers at my back. Pulling. As if she was trying to pull herself right out of that miserable existence. I knew she'd been abused when she was young but now I could actually feel it. Nothing: not the smell of drink, nor the stink of tobacco, nor stale sweat, nor the waft of pish could've stopped me giving her a cuddle. When I loosened my grip she held on more. Tighter and tighter. I tried to let go but she squeezed.

—Don't let me go, she kept saying, —Don't let me go.

A tear came out of me then cos I knew there was no way she was ever going to break free. I decided to hold her for as long as it took. Bruce Springsteen would have to wait.

After a minute I heard Jimmy crying. Jimmy the Hoover. The best Shoplifter in the West. A legend. Crying.

—What about me? he was saying. —What about me? I want a cuddle.

85

Kerry-Anne let me go.

—Give Jimmy a cuddle, she said. —Jimmy needs a cuddle.

Jimmy was over in the corner and his cheekbones were wet. I gave Joe a look as I passed. I don't know if he ever knew what that look meant. But I tried to say – sometimes there's things in life you've got to do Joe. Sometimes you've got to look over and beyond your prejudice and disgust and disappointment. Sometimes you've just got to love. But I don't think he got all that.

I took Jimmy and held onto him. Man drowning at sea. Jimmy had been sober a few years and we both knew what that meant. Some bit of him was trying to climb back out again. But it was all caving in. Tumbling.

—Everything's going to be alright Jimmy, I said. — Everything's going to be alright.

But I knew, and Jimmy knew, and everybody up that close knew everything wasn't going to be alright. Everything was going to be far from alright. Jimmy pushed me away, looked in my eyes and said,

—You better get out of here big man. This is no place for the likes of you.

—Don't you tell my brother what's good for him and what's not Hoover! Paul shouted.

—Don't hit him Jimmy, I whispered. —Not unless he hits you – then just do what's necessary.

Jimmy told me he'd look after Paul and kissed me on the cheek.

—Coming Joe? I said.

—Eh aye! He was and quick. Joe had that what-kind-of-a-crazy-place-is-this? look on his face when we were leaving the close. Then a pique of guilt made me turn, go back and thrust twenty quid in Paul's hand. He's going to get drink anyway and my figuring is the sooner he gets to where he can't take any more the better. Or maybe that's not it? Maybe that's me trying to moralise? To be the good guy. I think the truth of the twenty quid is more like this: I know what it's like to be choking for a drink and have no money. Paul took the twenty and was crying. This time the tears were real. But they turned from despair to anxiety to anger to aggression and he went for me. Lunged in with a big haymaker of a punch. It was a postcard job. I could've made a cup of tea as I waited for it to come over. I dodged sideways. Jimmy held him back and Paul started ranting.

—Embarrassed to walk down the main street with your brother?

—What? I said.

—Embarrassed to walk down the main street with your brother?

—Nobody said nothing about walking down no main street Paul.

But he kept repeating himself so I said. —Come on then, we'll walk down to The Fountain and back.

He spat on me. That was his answer to that.

—I'm not walking down no fuckin main street so you can show off that you're sober! Oh look at me everybody! I've been off the drink for ninety-five years!

He swung a punch and hit the wall. Danced about sucking his knuckles and blamed that on me too.

—Look what you've made me do, he kept shouting, look what you've made me do!

There was no talking to him. I decided it would be best if I went. Joe was hanging about the edge of the close not knowing to be embarrassed or not.

—I'm away, I said with no venom nor emotion that you

could detect.

—See ye later, said Jimmy.

—Thanks for the cuddle, said Kerry-Anne.

—It wasn't that when you were up this close with us ya prick! shouted Paul and ranted bringing up the past. I was nearly out the close when he shouted it.

—He's an alky Joe – did ye know that about your da? Eh? A dirty no good alky! He killed his best pal Joe, did ye know that? A punch Joe. One punch Joe. He's a murderer.

Jimmy the Hoover clamped his hand over Paul's mouth and dragged him backwards, nodding to me to escape. But it was too late. The word echoed along the close and fell drunk onto the main street. People were walking in an arc round about them. Jimmy and Kerry-Anne were giving Paul a hard time. As I left the close I could hear their voices lessen and lessen. It reminded me of something I had read recently in a book about Romans. Echo was a nymph who was in love with Narcissus. But when he didn't love her back she pined away till only her voice remained. Only now I couldn't tell if it was Paul pining away or me.

Out on the main street was a different world for me and Joe. The sun was shining and people went about their business. Joe sighed the way you do at the end of a blinding movie. Like the opening scene of *Saving Private Ryan* or Rutger Hauer's speech on the roof in *Blade Runner*.

—Come on Dad, we'll go and get that CD, he said. He never mentioned what Paul said. And he's never mentioned it since. We were lucky. We got the last *Greatest Hits* and I raved all the way back to the car about it. He got in just before me. I took a second to look at him and say a prayer or make a wish or whatever it is I do – that he'd not end up in the darkness of some close breaking his whole family's heart.

We drove off and at The Fountain I could see the close like a black hole in the brightness of the street. I watched it in my wing mirror till it was a dot and I wondered if I'd ever see my brother again. Joe turned the CD up full blast and The Boss sang loud and clear,

♪ Now them memories come back to haunt me, they haunt me like a curse. Is a dream a lie if it don't come true, or is it something worse, that sends me down to the river, though I know the river is dry...

Heat

The heat was unbearable. I couldn't sleep. And while I sat
sweating on the white sheets the old feeling came over me.
They were playing poker and didn't even turn when I slid
past. I pushed it and jumped in coasting to the gates where
I started the engine. Only turned on the lights when I was a
mile away.

By the time I got to the city it was three in the morning. I
had all the windows down but the air rushing in was still hot.
I was going back to my old street but I couldn't remember
where it was. My heart was beating with anticipation. But
there were so many new roads and buildings it didn't look
like my city at all. I stopped in a place with a multi-screen
cinema and a few eating joints. A bowling alley. McDonald's.
Frankie and Johnnies. The neons advertising to people who
weren't there. The interior lights on but nobody home. Like
everybody had left in a hurry. Like they knew I was coming.
I got out and stretched my legs. It was eerie. There wasn't a
drop of wind. The air was warm to touch. Only the odd rush
of a passing car on the motorway.

The odd rush of a passing car.

Other people driving through their own nights. Try as I
might I couldn't remember how to get back to that street.
The motorway and the giant signs meant nothing to me.

Then it came to me. Take the old way. The old roads. They must still be there.

And they were, the old roads. Still there. Silent and laid out before me, for me, with me, in me even. I took my hands off the steering wheel and the car soon had me back in that old street. Nothing had changed except the curtains. And the old streetlamps replaced by high silver sodium lamps, projecting orange balls of light on the tenements. I crept along looking for my house.

Although the rest of the civilised city was asleep here was alive. Women were hanging out of windows smoking. Their skin sodium yellow and the tips of their fags glowing as they watched me pass. I wondered if they were thinking about sex. There was this one girl about twenty-five and she was gorgeous. She had long dark hair. Long dark hair. Her head swung and followed me. And her hair followed.

Her hair followed.

Then – there it was. My house. Top flat. The windows were dark but I could see curtains. I wondered if they were the kind of curtains she would have. If she was still there? I remembered her look when they arrested me. It was one of disbelief. Total disbelief.

—Tell me it's not true, she said. I didn't say anything back. We had kids.

I could see the girl with the dark hair in my mirror. She was looking at me. Or maybe it was the car she was looking at. I couldn't tell you what kind it was but I think it was a good one. It was Patrick's and he was a bodybuilder with blonde hair and a big ego. An eye for the women too, like myself.

Then there was barking. A pack of dogs mobbed around a three year old boy. He was holding half a Mars bar above his head. Tormenting them. The dogs were growling and snapping at each other. Jumping up through that boy's laughter. And the boy's grin. And the boy's eyes. Narrow.

—Sit, said the boy.

Half the dogs sat. The others looked bewildered. Never having known discipline. Once he had all the dogs' attention the boy opened his mouth and lowered the Mars bar in. Chomped at the dogs. Like he knew their language of saliva and mouth. I could smell the bad feeling in that pack of dogs. The boy threw the wrapper into them. An instant boiling mass of barking fur. And him walking round the outside kicking and shouting.

—Kill! Kill!

My pyjamas were drenched in sweat.

Everybody in that street turned at the same time. Even the dogs. There was a man arguing with his wife. They had obviously been to a wedding. He had a suit with a withered carnation and she had a ludicrous purple dress. By their sweeping movements I could see they were drunk. He pushed her against the wall. The thump of her head. The delicious thump of her head. The woman was sliding down. People at windows had to lean out to the waist. The man dragged her upright and shouted into her face. His mouth is big and violent. Like the cops who questioned me. She's terrified, the woman, terrified. I drove closer to that terror. Nobody noticed at five miles an hour. When I got there he banged her head off the wall again. She flopped like a rag doll.

—You're a hoor Mary int ye?

—No Tommy I'm not.

—Just tell me the truth Mary – you're a wee hoor int ye?

—I've never been near another man Tommy, honest!

This time his knees were bent and he had her by the

93

throat. Lifting her up. I could hear the notes of strangulation.

—Say you're a hoor and I'll leave ye alone.

—No Tommy, you'll kill me.

—I won't – just say it.

He let her down off her toes. There was a pause then she said it.

—Okay – Tommy, I'm a wee hoor.

Tommy's hand lifted so slowly it could be Tai Chi.

—Aye – I knew ye were a wee hoor.

Bang. He punched her. She folded. I could see her thighs. Her thighs.

I don't know how he sensed me but he turned. My pyjamas were drenched with sweat. The closer he got the slower he walked. About ten feet from the car another man appeared and knocked Tommy out. One punch. Folded like wet spaghetti.

—D'you get some kinda kick beating up women?

But that's all he got to say cos Mary jumped on this man's back punching and screaming. Dragging her nails across his face.

—That's my Man – leave my Man alone ya bastard!

He swept her off. Held her out of kicking distance until Tommy recovered enough to hear his new instructions.

—Hit her again and you're a dead man.

Tommy nodded his understanding. The man left him in a pool of fear. Mary helped Tommy to his feet. Arm in arm they staggered away.

They got the boy away from the dogs and took him inside. It was my house the light came on in. The boy appeared at a window with a slice of bread. And I could see them arguing in the living room. Tommy was pointing at her and shouting. She shouted back and turned away, came to the window and looked out then turned and shouted at him. I remembered my wife standing in roughly the same position the night the cops burst in. I was on the couch. I wanted arrested. Craved arrest. But that was a long time ago. Before my craving outstripped my guilt.

When the telly came crashing through the window and detonated on the street the dogs exploded in all directions. From a window somewhere there came applause. The girl with the black hair lit another cigarette and blew smoke in my direction. Blew smoke

in my direction.

I drove with the lights off to the next street and went in through the back greens. She was still leaning out the window when I pulled her backwards. Later, I drove back to the ward and nobody knew I was gone. The next day it would be in all the papers.

The Illustrated Man

Mickey Maclehatton got murdered by his two wine buddies. Took turns stabbing him, rolled him in a carpet and dragged him over the railway. Set him on fire to destroy the evidence. They're doing life now these two guys; in separate jails. But truth be told it could've been any one of them that night. They were forever attacking each other with blades. It was only a matter of time cos three alkies living together is a recipe for murder.

But Mickey wasn't always a jakie. He'd lived with his da, Paddy, and his brother, Stevie. Had a bird and a job and a nice wee motor. But one day his bird ditched him for a guy from the posh end of town. That's when Mickey sat on the slippery slope and gave himself a wee push. Nothing monumental. But he was on his way down.

His brother Stevie had no job, no bird and no motor. To compound that he had a gammy left leg and a busted left arm. Even though nobody in that house was admitting it, Stevie wasn't the full fifty pence. So as Mickey accelerated down that slippery slope, Stevie's joy increased. His best day was when Stevie sold him the motor for three hundred quid. Mickey was out there night and day T-Cutting and polishing. No matter that he couldn't drive.

—Like my new motor? he said to passers by. On top of

that Stevie always managed to get you to ask how was Mickey.

—What that jakie? That alkie bastard? This good for nothing fuckin waster?

And he'd run his brother down so that it was embarrassing. If he wasn't polishing another thin skin of paint off that car, he'd sit fiddling with the radio. Tilt the seats back and doze. Even seen him out there in the middle of the night with a flask of coffee. Maybe he thought: car equals women and they would flock to him. But he'd no chance. He was an ugly bastard.

Then one day the car wasn't there.

—Where's your motor the day then Stevie boy? I says.

—Our Mickey drove it away in the middle of the night and mashed it into a bus.

And he made it sound like Mickey's done it on purpose; crash the car I mean. Well, sure enough three days after that here's the bold Mickey with more plaster than a Michelangelo sculpture being teetered up the garden path by two paramedics. Like a big white Frankenstein. From that day on, by all accounts, Stevie never spoke to Mickey again. In his life.

He got worse and worse did Mickey, and Stevie was forever trying to persuade their da to fling him out. Then he stole the spending money Stevie and his da'd saved up for Tenerife. They only noticed it was gone the day they were leaving. They spent two weeks living on fruit on the beach. And picking black sand out their toes at night while the whole island partied. Paddy'd no choice. When they came back home they changed the locks.

Three months after that Mickey was dead. It was a wee while before they got his body home, with the post mortem and the trial and all that. The Diamond was surprised when they buried Mickey out of Paddy's house. And even more surprised at the state Stevie was in. He was distraught the boy. Breaking down for this brother he hated his whole life. Everybody thought he was putting it on.

But I spoke to Stevie at the rosary and it was all our Mickey this and our Mickey that.

—Our Mickey was great so he was. The best. He was some guy. I don't think nobody on The Diamond appreciated that.

I agreed with him and slipped away, left him praising Mickey up to Franny Flanagan.

Time passed and whereas before you avoided Stevie cos he hated his brother now you avoided him cos he loved him. Six every morning he walked three miles to the graveyard. Said Hail Marys over Mickey's grave and swore revenge on the two that murdered him. Of course he wasn't going to see them for a long time. But rage and bitterness needs somewhere to go. It wasn't long before Stevie turned it on his da. Made that old man's life misery. Accused him of murdering Mickey by flinging him out of the house.

—He wouldn't be dead if you let him stay here.

—It was you that wanted me to put him out. Ye went on and on and on. D'you think it's easy to put your own son out on the street?

Words come back and often haunt. Cos did the same argument not take place a few days later? Stevie accuses his da of murdering Mickey. His da goes mental and attacks Stevie. Stevie hits his da on the head with a big ornament. So for the second time in a bad year Paddy Maclehatton puts a son on the street. That had the effect of pushing Stevie's hate outwards.

Social work got him a house. Right in the heart of the Diamond. Straight across from me. He'd been an oddity before but now I could see something else in him. People kept telling me not to be daft, to mind my own business. But fear's got this way of making me obsessed so I kept an eye on Stevie Maclehatton.

Once he'd settled in he took to running round the football park a hundred times a day. Anti-clockwise because of his gammy leg and arm. Every centrifugal lap sent his resentment out further so that within a month he hated the whole Diamond.

Then, on a cold morning in March, it took a turn for the worse. Seven o'clock and the street lights still on and there he was lapping that park, his feet crunching through icy puddles. But there was something different. There was something printed on his T-shirt. I got the binoculars.

Paddy Maclehatton is a murdering bastard

It was big black letters and by the time he'd ran fifty laps the whole Diamond knew about it. I'm sure Paddy Maclehatton knew too. Stevie wore that to the doctors for his sick line. To ASDA for his messages. Passing his da's a dozen times to my reckoning. Hovering about the gate making a big show of tying his laces or reading the clouds. People thought it was terrible. Old Paddy was seventy.

He wore it night and day for over a week. With the running and the hate seeping out he was rank. You could smell him ten feet away. One night he tried to get into the club. Paddy was playing dominoes and could see the commotion at the door. Even though nobody at that table acknowledged what was going on there was a change in him. When he put down the double six something had flew away from Paddy Maclehatton. He'd lost two sons with one blow. He pushed his pint away.

—The drink's a cunt, he said and till Stevie killed him he never touched another drop.

Meanwhile the bouncers were giving Stevie an almighty kicking. All the time moralising about that T-shirt. Stevie knelt there laughing. Blood running out his mouth.

—Kick me again. Kick me again, he kept saying.

When they wouldn't he started punching himself hard in the face. They left him punching his bust lips laughing through red stalactites of bloody saliva.

Paddy Maclehatton started going to daily mass with his sister Cathy. She was one of the hangovers from the Irish invasion six generations ago who carried on the old ways. Daily duties and a certain way of living that had long since died out on the homeland.

Time passed. The T-shirt was being forgotten when there he was, crashing through the daffodils, their yellow dust round his ankles and something new on his T-shirt.

Cathy Maclehatton
sucks dicks

People had gathered by the pitch staring daggers but Stevie kept running. Faster than ever. Like he was trying to burst his own heart. Even when they started shouting abuse he kept going. When he was finished he walked through them taking their insults like passing flies. Right up The Diamond with 'Cathy Maclehatton sucks dicks'.

He wore that for over a week. The Diamond was not pleased. All sorts of people were saying things to him now.

—That's out of order that, so it is.

—Have you no shame?

—That's an oul lady that.

—She's every day at mass so she is that woman, God forgive ye!

Eventually Father Kelly came to see him. But Stevie threatened him with a T-shirt of his own and Father Kelly backed off.

Stevie started telling people it was The Diamond that killed his brother. But people just smiled and said ach don't be silly Stevie. But he was more than silly. He was fuckin dangerous. But would they listen to me? No – would they fuck! His next T-shirt said

The Diamond
is getting it

This time, as he lapped, the odd rock was flung in with the insults. Timmy Gallagher scudded him on the arse with a Buckie bottle. But nothing. He just kept going. People got fed up threatening him and went about their own business.

Then, in the autumn, people in The Diamond started taking ill. Randomly. A lot ending up in hospital. First of all the doctors thought it was maybe food poisoning. But it was happening so regular they investigated. They found all sorts in the bellies – Vim, soap powder, sperm, spit, petrol, diesel, glass, paracetamol, on and on the list went. These people had one thing in common. They'd all had a meal from the Lucky Dragon. Environmental Health bought, over a week, a

THE ILLUSTRATED MAN

hundred meals, and found nothing.

It was only when Franny Flanagan got his Chicken Cashew nuts fried rice delivered and ran out cos they'd forgot his prawn crackers that we realised. There, in the back of the delivery driver's mobility Corsa was Stevie Maclehatton. The driver was from another scheme and knew nothing about Stevie's T-shirts and his war with The Diamond. When the cops questioned the driver he said there'd been a spate of curries getting nicked from the car. Stevie came up one day and started a conversation about the curry thief. Offered to come out and guard the meals while the driver goes to the doors. For nothing. For free. The driver thought Stevie might just be lonely. Looking for something to do. The cops knew and I knew and The Diamond knew Stevie was filling them wee boxes with all sorts of poison when the driver was out the car. But there was nothing they could do. There was no proof. The Diamond was angry.

There was whispers about doing something. The whispers turned to meetings and a decision was made. When he appeared the next morning with his latest T-shirt

The Diamond Dies

there was thirty or forty people waiting. Men and women. Old and young. We kicked pure seven bells of Hell out Stevie Maclehatton.

It was only when Paul Brennan put the noose round his neck and tried to haul him up a lamp post that we stopped. We left him crumpled on the pavement.

—Merry Christmas, said Paul Brennan and kicked him once as he left. We set fire to Stevie's house on the way home. Nobody watched it burn.

People were shocked to see his obituary in the *Advertiser* a few days later.

Please pray for the repose of the soul of Stephen Maclehatton. Tragically removed from this Earth 21st December 2005. Stephen will be Sadly missed by his father Patrick, his Aunt Catherine and by all in The Diamond. RIP.

They say when Paddy read it he just shook his head. Then his face loosened with relief. But his relief turned instantly to grief.

And shock waves ran through The Diamond. We waited for the cops to come. Worried about just whose kick or punch killed him. Or maybe he'd got back in that house before we set fire to it? But there was no cops. No black van. No body. People flung accusations at each other. Fought and fragmented. But the cops never came. And The Diamond steadily drank its worry away through the festive period. If there was ever a funeral we never heard a peep about it.

On the third of January when we were all nursing hangovers the word went up that Stevie Maclehatton, or his waft, was jogging round the football pitch. We filed down to see this apparition. Sure enough, there he was jogging as fast as ever through January frost.

With a new T-shirt

I'm a ghost
Whooooo!

The crowd fell even more silent when Paddy arrived. He took one look and walked away. Stevie never acknowledged us at all. Even when the cops arrested him. Questioned him for days trying to find his motivation for announcing his own

104

death. But there was no insurance claim, nothing they could connect to a crime. Seemingly it's not illegal to announce your own death. They had to let him go.

Stevie Maclehatton took to living in his burnt out shell of a house as if there was nothing amiss. Boiling the buckled kettle and making tea in a cracked teapot. Sitting on a charcoaled chair by the burnt table. His fingers black and soot specks on his teeth.

The council came and forced him into an empty flat two doors down. First thing he done was paint all the windows black. The council said there was nothing they could do about that – he wasn't harming anybody. Nobody seen him for months but we knew he was in there.

In the first cold sun of spring he stood by his gate and whipped the T-shirt off so we could all read his masterpiece.

He spotted me with the binoculars and turned. Slowly. Deliberately. Every sentence. Every word. Every crazy little drawing tattooed with the most lurid colours of ink. The story of Mickey's murder. The T-shirt slogans. New abuse. Old abuse. It was all there if you cared to look. And he went that whole summer rain hail or shine with just a pair of shorts. Got ejected from ASDA and stood outside for eight hours. Kids shouted abuse, the alkies pelted him with empty cans, a few Neds slapped him about. But still he stood; the illustrated man.

On the morning they found Paddy Maclehatton dead there was a commotion outside. I rushed out with my jeans flung on. Up and down the street people were walking with their heads down.

Follow the arrows >>>>>>>>

There was lines of arrows starting in every outreach of The Diamond. Snaking in and out closes and cars, crossing roads, going up garden paths and back out again. But they all eventually converged on one point.

When I got to Paddy Maclehatton's there was a crowd. The cops had been phoned and Franny Flanagan was shouting through the letter box. But there was no answer. Somebody shouted could he smell anything? He took a long sniff. Nothing. Then Cathy Maclehatton arrived. With a key. The crowd parted and in she went.

It was silent. Like an overcrowded wake. Then a scream. Some people ran in. Two came out holding Cathy up. One of them was sick in the hedges. The cops arrived and cleared us all away. But not before Franny Flanagan and Joe McGhee had a right good look.

The walls were covered with computer printouts. Each one dated. Stevie Maclehatton's diary. A day by day blow of his growing hatred. His da was stripped bare and tied up. Mickey's name was carved out on his skin in as many sizes and places you can imagine. They said he'd bled to death from the cuts. That he'd felt every point of piercing, every unzipping cut of skin. Mickey put all his emotions into his father's skin.

It was reported in the papers as a one-off bizarre incident. But it was hard to see how they didn't see that coming. I seen it coming. We all seen it. We'd reported him to the cops, the council, the social work, the MSPs the MPs. But what did they do? Fuck all! Jesus, all we had to do was follow the arrows.

Gold Roman Coins

Me and John got hounded out of town. They gave John a right doing and when he staggered into my house covered in blood they crashed all my windows in. We got ourselves under the bed but they flung in a petrol bomb and we had to get out of there. I ran out first swinging the spade like an ancient Celtic axe and cleared a path.

—Come on John, run, I shouted, —Run like fuck.

But they set about him. The women were the worst. I got as many as I could with the spade but then I was on the deck with boots raining in like applause. Next thing I remember is the clothes being ripped off me. Then me and John being marched down Potato Road in the nude. Surrounded by a taunting crowd. Glass particles sticking in my feet. Now and then somebody would hit us or one of the women would run up and spit in my face. Or John's. I tried to tell them it wasn't us. We wouldn't've done that. Not me and John. I can see now that whoever did do it was probably in that crowd. But every time you opened your mouth you got a punch. John's teeth were bleeding. I hadn't cried all through it. But when I seen John's new van in flames I started bubbling. When they got us to the edge of town as many of them that could booted our arses and flung what was left of our clothes at us. Me and John ran away from the Haste Ye Back sign in a shower of missiles, holding our clothes like babies.

It was my fault. If I hadn't bought that metal detector, none of it would've happened. One wet Tuesday afternoon I was flicking through my catalogue wondering what I could pay up out of my Social Security when there it was. One-fifty a week for a hundred weeks. It said it could differentiate between iron and precious metals. Find Buried Treasure, it said. There was a photo of a man with a bag of Gold Roman coins. He had a tan and white teeth. And a big cheesy it's-nice to-be-rich smile. It was the early eighties and most people were getting money stripping lead and copper from the closed down steelworks.

At first I wasn't going to buy it. Everybody knew the Romans never got into Scotland. We kicked the shit out of them, so what was the point in a metal detector? I was telling John about it and he laughed. He'd read a lot of books in the jail. The Romans was one of his subjects. He said he'd bring me a map and some books after he'd took his lead to Hanna's. And off he went pushing a wheelbarrow with sheets of lead crushed into it. I was thinking he might get ten or fifteen quid for that – and that's nearly a hundred a week if he goes up the Klondike every day. If he did he'd soon have his van. It was five hundred quid the van. On display in the forecourt in Wilson's and every time John passed he kissed his hand and slapped the kiss onto the roof.

—You're my wee baby, he'd say, —Daddy's coming to get ye. The salesman would shout did he have enough money yet and John would shout back,

—Getting there big man. Getting there.

—Better hurry up John before it gets snapped up, the salesman would say, —Goes like a wee sweetie this van.

And John was getting there. It was a slow but certain

way to make money; stripping the lead. I was tempted to abandon the whole metal detector idea, steal a wheelbarrow and go up on the Klondike roof myself. That night I wandered about looking for a wheelbarrow but there was none. People were keeping them in their houses. But anyway, I took one look at the height of the Klondike roof and realised copper and lead would never really make you rich. What you needed was gold. That's the fellah there. Gold Roman coins lit up the inside of my head like rows of yellow streetlights. The cops drew up and asked what I was doing.

—Just wandering about officer, I said. —Can't sleep.

They drew me a suspicious look and got out the car. Then I noticed a bunch of the Finnegans. The cops went over and I could see the Finnegans were crying. Weeping in fact. Holding each other up. A few of the neighbours consoling them. I asked McGinty what was up. Had somebody died?

—Worse, he said.

What could be worse than that? I was thinking when he told me. Their son Peter died last month. He'd been ten years in the Klondike and never missed a shift. He was programmed. Wasn't much of a drinker so he still had three grand left long after we'd all drank our redundancy. Or gambled it. But he was depressed. Lack of work was killing him. He'd never had nothing to do before. And nothing to worry about. He'd done every job he could in the house and garden and then took to his bed and didn't get back up. Nothing and nobody could coax him. When he hung himself from the rafters he was just turned twenty-seven. His maw blamed the Klondike. If he was still there he'd have went automatic to work every day and came home via the Wire Inn for one exact pint every night. He'd watch his programmes and go to bed.

At his wake, just before they screwed the coffin lid down his maw kissed him on the head.

—Your granny'll look after ye son, is what she said and she produced two big wads of notes and put them in the coffin. It was the last two grand of his redundancy money.

—Take this with ye son, she said. —That's what killed ye.

But now somebody had dug up the grave, burst open the coffin, dragged his decomposing body out and took the money. Left Peter Flanagan sitting against the muddy sides looking at the smashed up lid of his own coffin. A couple of Neds with some dope came across it and ran screaming all the way to the cop station. All I could say was fucksakes. McGinty went back over to the Finnegans. I left the street with Mrs Finnegan wailing for revenge.

The next day John brought me round a couple of books and a big map. I told him about Peter Finnegan's grave and he said he'd heard. It was all round the town. That was all they were talking about on the roof. Finnegan, even though he never drank much, was a well liked guy. Well respected.

—Whoever done it's a dead man if it ever comes out, said John.

It was giving us the fear so we decided not to talk about it any more. We got into the books. He showed me Antonine's wall on the map and bits of the book telling us where the Romans had camped. I never knew they'd got so far into Scotland. At first I was angry but John laughed.

—It was thousands of years ago ya dick, he said, —Ye might even be a Roman yourself the size of that nose.

And he pointed out that I should be happy. For all I knew the Romans had been in Greenend. For all I know they'd even camped under my house. For all I know there was bags of Gold Roman coins in the back garden. John had me

convinced. I had to get the metal detector. He offered me
a partnership on the Klondike roof. He could rip the lead
off and I could barrow it to Hanna's. But my stomach was
churning for the metal detector.

I was in the phone box early next morning. At exactly one
minute after nine I phoned the catalogue. I spoke as posh as
I could because sometimes when they heard your accent they
wouldn't send the stuff. The woman was nice enough and
chatted a bit about what I was going to do with the treasure.
I think I went on too much about living south of Antonine's
wall and the Romans having camped all over the place and
who knows they might even have camped in my back garden.
As soon as there was a break she cut in, said it would be
twenty-one days delivery and hung up.

It was going to be a long twenty-one days and I felt a bit
depressed. I couldn't even look at the catalogue. I wanted it
now. I was even going to phone back and ask exactly where
the metal detector was at this precise moment in time. It
must be in England somewhere and I could hitch-hike or
jump the trains and pick it up. That's hardly going to take
more than three days. I got John's maps out and looked at
places in England where metal detectors might be. Bath
looked like a good spot. Or London. Londinium it was on
the maps in the books. Londinium. I bet they make metal
detectors there. It didn't look that far on the map.

John came round. He showed me a hundred quid. Let me
hold it. It felt good having so much money in my hand but
it made me feel a bit sick. He gave me a tenner and crashed
open a can of super lager. I told him how I felt about the
metal detector not coming for three weeks and he helped
me. Said I should spend the time planning. Where I was going
to go. Where the treasure was most likely to be. He was right.

I decided to spend the time constructively. John had to go.
He was meeting his brother Wullie who was just out the jail.
John was determined to keep him on the straight and narrow
and was going to offer him the partnership in the lead-
stealing business. He checked I still didn't want it and left.

I got an old calendar, scored out all the wrong day names
and wrote in the right ones. I counted forwards twenty-one
days and started scribbling in where I would go and what
I would do. What I would wear. What I would have to eat.
My plan was to go along Antonine's wall and search under
all the bits that had been forts. If I was a Roman soldier and
I wanted to bury treasure – I'd walk away from the fort till
I couldn't be seen because of a hill or some other obstacle.
Bury my treasure there. I looked on the map for hillocks
near forts and located two right away. I started to feel really
excited. I spent a few days planning and dreaming about
treasure. First thing I would do is buy John his van. He's been
good to me John since my maw died. I went to bed reading a
book about Romans in Scotland.

The Antonine Wall goes across Britain from the Firth of
Forth to the Firth of Clyde. Built of turf on a stone foundation
as a barrier against the Picts and Caledonians, the wall is 10
feet high, 14 to 16 feet wide, and will have 13 to 19 forts
along its 37-mile length.

Nineteen forts! Boy was I going to plunder that Antonine's
Wall. I noticed there was another Roman camp not far from
here. To the east. I folded the big map out on the bed and
compared it to the old one in John's book. Kirk O Shotts it
was called. I made a note to go there after I had drained
Antonine's wall of every Gold Roman coin it had.

John came round crying a few days later. I thought
somebody had bought the van but it was Wullie. He was

back in the jail. A couple of plain clothes cops came up on the roof in the morning and joined in. Nobody knew them but they looked hard so everybody let them get on with it. When everybody stopped for a tea break the two cops grabbed Wullie and cuffed him. A couple of cop cars appeared out of nowhere and some guys who'd been lifting cast iron drainers ran over. They were undercover cops too. They had it in for Wullie cos when he got lifted for the armed robbery he stabbed a cop. They wanted to run him out of town. They weren't that bothered about the lead and in fact they told they guys to go back soon as they were gone. Wullie got two years and I'll never forget that day because that's the day my metal detector came.

I came home from Airdrie Sheriff with John and there was a card to pick it up at the post office. John went to get drunk but I had tunnel vision for this metal detector. When I got it home I ripped the box open and savoured that new smell. It had been a long time since something new was in my house. It was batteries not included but I already bought them weeks ago. Two sets and I shoved one of them in. It buzzed away like a wee dalek. I started swinging it about the house. It made a great noise over the pots. I flung the keys under the carpet – found them every time. I done it with my eyes shut and it found them. I waved it over door handles, found nails in walls, pipes in the toilet, the telly even. If you were metal there was nowhere to hide. Then I remembered the promise in the catalogue, repeated on the outside of the box, that this particular model could differentiate between precious and other metals. I had a gold ring my maw gave me and put that down. Man! What a delight. It made this other great noise for gold. A wee happy buzz.

In the garden all I dug up was nails, old car bits and a

washing machine lid in very bad condition. But that didn't bother me. I was on. I was away. I'd be rich soon and couldn't wait to surprise John with his wee van.

Two days later John was visiting Wullie in Shotts jail. He had to get a train and three buses. It was an all day job and he was always knackered when he came back. He asked me if I wanted to go. Wullie had got my name put on the pass. But I had my rucksack and spade and metal detector and I was off to Antonine's wall.

—Sorry John, I said. —I'll go the next time but.

The bus dropped me off in the middle of nowhere. I walked for half an hour to the first spot I had marked. There was nobody about and it felt good to be up on the moors after the claustrophobia of Greenend. Always people watching from windows.

Talk about beginner's luck. I went to the fort, closed my eyes and imagined I was a Roman soldier with treasure to hide. I walked away pretending all these other sneaky bastards of Romans were watching. I walked round this little hillock and stood out of sight. To the right was a rocky point and behind me was the hill. A stream ran down. I lined the three things up and walked to that very spot. I started to swing the metal detector. It buzzed. And not just the any-old-iron buzz. It buzzed the precious metal buzz. I expected it to be a ring and don't get me wrong, I was excited. First day out, first search and a gold ring. One of them a day and I'd be rich in jig time. I dug and sifted through the soil. Nothing. Swung the detector. It buzzed again, only this time a lot happier. I dug down and came to a slate. It had obviously been placed there. I sifted carefully round about it climbing onto the hillock now and then to check for people. When I lifted the slate my face fell. I had found a small pile of dirt just. But when I lifted it out what had been a leather bag disintegrated and all these gold coins came shining through. Tumbling over my fingers. I was so excited I had to turn away and be sick. I was shaking. When I got my act together I stuffed the coins into my pockets, filled the hole up, flung the slate in the burn and got out of there quick.

On the way back the driver kept asking if I was alright. I gave him one word answers but you could see he was suspicious. He was noting every detail in case any bodies were found up near Antonine's wall. You don't probably get a lot of guys with spades on his bus. And I had the metal detector in a black bin bag so that nobody knew what I was up to. I didn't even dare move in case the coins jangled. I sat bolt upright all the way over them country roads to Airdrie. I walked it home feeling like Wullie must feel when he's done a successful robbery. Elated, sick, and paranoid that somebody's going to ask me to turn my pockets out.

When I got home I counted out seventeen gold coins. Sat them in rows. In piles. All flat on the table. Ran the metal detector over them and thrilled at that precious buzz. I knew not to contact anybody official. They would just take them off me. I waited for John but when he never came round I figured he must've been too tired and upset after the visit.

But by half-three in the morning I couldn't take any more and went round. I passed Mrs Finnegan at her window and waved but I don't think she seen me. John wasn't a happy bunny when I climbed in his side window and woke him up.

—What the fuck is with you? he said, rubbing his eyes and scratching his balls. I shouted taa naa and showered the coins on his bed. He picked one up turning it one side to the other, weighing it in his hand. Reading the inscription. Lighting up more and more. John knew his Romans cos he spouted

off the year and the emperor and where they came from.
He even knew a guy who would buy them no questions. He
couldn't sleep now. He got up and got ready.

We walked it into Glasgow and he was telling me he
had two hundred and fifty quid. He needed the same again
to get the wee van. Then he could start his own business
delivering or window cleaning or whatever. After he'd got
the last of the lead off the Klondike. I wasn't daft. I knew he
wanted me to give him the rest of the money for the van, so
I told him I would and I swear he picked up his step. We had
a breakfast in a wee all-nighter in Dennistoun then walked
to the West End. I'd never been in the West End before and
couldn't believe the big posh houses and fancy cars. I thought
the country was in recession but it didn't look like it here.
Beautiful women were coming out to take shiny kids to
school. We came to a house in a street with trees and a wee
park that said Private on it. John told me to wait at the end
of the park.

As I waited I tried to figure how much the coins were
worth. Might be hundreds. Could be thousands. A Mercedes
went past and the woman glared at me. I decided to walk
up and down so as not to draw attention to myself. But I
couldn't help looking in. There was furniture I'd only seen
on the telly. Fancy curly mirrors and leather couches. Who
knows, maybe the coins are worth millions? I built this picture
of me rich and was practically moving into the West End
when John came back.

He had a thousand pounds. I suppose I should've been
happy but I wasn't. I thought it would be better. Even so I
gave John three hundred. Two hundred and fifty for the car
and fifty for himself. We went into Argyle street and bought
new clothes. The works – shoes, socks, underwear, jeans and

jumpers. I got a haircut and we threw our old clothes up a lane full of tramps. John said not to mention the coins to nobody. They guy we sold them to was heavy. If we grassed him up – he'd kill us. Simple as that.

When we got back home we looked a million dollars. Everybody was commenting on how good we looked. Asking us if we won the pools. John told them we won on the horses and down we went to Wilson's. You should've seen John when he bought that wee van. It was the happiest I've ever seen him. When we parked outside his house Mrs Finnegan was still at her window. It was as if she was waiting for her Peter to come home. We waved politely and she waved a wee half-wave. Then she stared at John's van with a look I couldn't fathom at the time.

Three days later in the pub the talk was all about this money we won. He's a clever man John; when they asked him what his bet was he rhymed it off good style. It was a three cross treble and he named the horses. Sure enough they had won at the right odds for the fifty quid lead money John said he put on along with my fifty quid stake.

Except. John hadn't reckoned on one of the Finnegans going to the betting shop and threatening the manager. By the time he got back to the pub me and John were off to visit Wullie. And it was true. John's van did go like a wee sweetie.

On the way home from Shotts I spied a sign. Kirk O Shotts.

—John that's the place on the map. There used to be a big Roman encampment there. Pull in.

He stopped at this wall surrounding an ancient graveyard and an old church. I jumped over first and he handed me the metal detector. I laid it on the grass. There were a couple of old trees at the other end and I felt sure there was gold under them. I felt lucky. I leaned back up and John was just handing me the spade over when McGinty went past in a car. He'd been visiting his wee brother in Shotts too. We waved but he never waved back. He just gunned the engine into the bend and up onto the M8. I can see now what he must've thought. He turns the corner and there's me behind a graveyard wall, John handing me a shovel and the back doors of the wee van open. It was getting dark and there was nobody about.

There was no gold under the big trees. We searched till it was too dark to see anything. I figured our luck had ran out and we went. John dropped me off at my house and went home. When he got in the lights wouldn't work. They beat him round the house. I thought I saw people in my garden. I put it down to tiredness. But they were there for me.

Heatherstone's Question

The two Heatherstone brothers, Pat and Matt, had a farm on a hill in Galloway above the Doon O May. On a good day you could see Ireland where they supposed they must have came from sometime back in history. It was rocky land and apart from the three fields they had mostly sheep and a few old cows that seemed to be part of the family. None of them ever got married and even if Pat was ugly as sin, Matt was a film star. You hardly ever seen them off the farm. Except for the Celtic games on a Saturday and chapel on Sunday. Pat, probably cos of his ugliness, never spoke to nobody. Matt sometimes chatted but his head was always on the farm, always on what was to be done next. They both made sure all the work on the farm was done by Saturday so they could go to the games.

Sometimes Matt would need to borrow things. Diesel. Silage. Tools. Four times a year at most Matt would come down to Willie McGaw's farm to ask a favour. McGaw's farm was on better land. Not great but enough to make it more prosperous. Willie McGaw would look out the window at Matt moving down the hill step by step, bit by bit.

—Here's oul Matt coming, stick the kettle on. Willie McGaw would shout to Annie, —Get the biscuits out.

Matt Heatherstone would chap the door, take a step

back, and stand with his blue eyes pleading and his big hands clasped together. Like somebody holy. An overgrown altar boy. Willie would come out and not far behind him, Annie with the tea and biscuits. Matt would stand at the door drinking the tea and rolling the biscuit over in his fingers, catching a glimpse now and then of the imposing kitchen table surrounded by who knows how many chairs. He never went inside the McGaw farmhouse. Never wanted to intrude. So he'd be chewing the cud all about the weather or the harvest. That's the way he was.

—Aye, mm hmm, aye you're right there sir, right enough. You're right there so ye are. Willie would be going, nodding away at Matt.

It was the same every time Matt came down. He'd be an infinity nibbling and then come away with something like,

—Any chance of a lend of some diesel Willie? We've ran out.

Sometimes it was just a few slice of bread just that he wanted. Matt was shy and Willie respectful. So if he was wanting a loaf till the shops opened on Monday he might talk about his dogs for an hour and then ask for a few wee slices of bread to shove him into Monday.

—Ye couldn't see your way to a couple of slice of bread to shove me and Pat into Monday Willie could ye?

And he'd get a loaf forever.

—Forget Monday cos bread's for sharing, Willie'd say.

Matt and Pat helped with muscle whenever he needed it. Through the years they helped, man and boy. Especially after all the McGaw boys, Rangers fans to a man, had left the farm for better things.

That's the way it went for years.

And years.

And years.

Every Saturday, at the bottom of the single track road, Matt and Pat would wish Willie good luck and he'd return the wish. They'd tip their hats and go their separate ways. Matt and Pat to meet the Celtic bus and Willie to meet the Rangers bus. By January 2001 Celtic were already running away with the league and Rangers were in a bit of a mess after a long time ruling Scottish football.

By February the snowdrops were up all over the hillside like white lace over green velvet. The blue sky soared overhead and the sun was orange in the morning and orange again in the evening. But this was the afternoon and the sun was yellow and oh so cold. There was a bit of a wind and the snowdrops' bowed heads were twisting uphill, straining in the gusts. Then falling back. Straining and falling back. Like they were watching Matt Heatherstone pressing through the Galloway winter. The wind was strong from the west and Matt could taste the Irish sea. Now and then the Mountains of Mourne appeared like history and were gone. Obscured by distant clouds. On he went, down the hill, his feet sinking through the gauze of snowdrops and rising; the leather flecked with pellets of water. As he stepped past, the flowerheads seemed to be following the passing away of his boots as the wind flared up and died for a moment. Their heads swung, like they were admiring themselves because today Matt's boots were shining like mirrors. The snowdrops seen their whiteness transfigured in a moment's consciousness and – whoom – were left trembling in the waft of his boots, the earthquake of his soles.

He'd not been down for six months. Willie came out to meet him as usual and Matt stood at the gate talking about summer then falling quiet. Willie was wondering what he was wanting but said nothing. In the silence, the poetry of the morning curved over Heatherstone's eyes. Glistening. Brighter than usual. Matt stood on the path and spoke about autumn.

—Brings ye nothing but bad luck that, a wet autumn, nothing but bad luck so it does.

Willie noticed there was something beneath Matt's words. The ever so ordinary words. Willie McGaw was moving backwards all the time, slow and imperceptible, but backwards just the same. By this time the tea had been handed out, and the biscuits. Backwards Willie McGaw was going all the time, sipping his tea and drawing Matt Heatherstone with him in the gravity of respect. Pulling him through the electromagnetic field of Matt's words still hanging in the air in front of his face like fog. Matt's wee words with greatness in them. Willie felt a mighty pang of sorrow, or grief, or something he'd not had since his sons started leaving. Here was a sudden and incredible empathy with Matt. He wished he could see more of this man, that they had been closer all the years they lived next to one and other. Then he realised they were at the door. The threshold that had never been crossed. Even if Matt was a Catholic and Willie a Protestant that was only half the reason the door had never been breached. They never knew what was in each other's houses. Till now. Heatherstone stood at the door and talked about winter, how it overlays the skin, flows into the lungs and burrows deep to the bones. Beneath his words of frost and ice was a shining coldness. A stillness. A clarity writers would die for.

—Will ye come in?

—I will, said Matt. —For a wee minute.

It was only the snowdrops swinging in the wind with their

heads bowed like reverence that witnessed Heatherstone
from the top of the hill entering the inner sanctuary of the
farm at the bottom of the hill. McGaw's farm. Matt took off
his cap and walked onto the altar of everyday life. Moved
into the tabernacle of kitchen. A nod towards Annie as she
said hello and turned away to save him awkwardness.

Matt sat at the fire looking mostly at the flames and
wondering what they were. Flames? They leap from the
dead peat, dance a crazy jig and then – there's nothing. Just
a dark space where the flame used to be. Matt bent forward
rubbing his hands, now and then holding them flat towards
the fire even though he wasn't feeling the cold. Willie was in
his rocking chair stuffing his pipe. Nothing was said. Nothing
was said for a long time. It was only the sounds of Annie in
the kitchen, the intermittent creak of the rocking chair and
the lick of the fire as the flames sheened over the surface
of their faces. And the tick of the clock. They were calm and
they were patient. It might have seemed like a long time to
you or me but sometimes we underestimate the peace that
can be found in silence. We've lost the knowledge of the
relativity of waiting.

And waiting.

And waiting.

But in Galloway, waiting is an art form. Every person a
lesson in meditation. A contemplation. Life is oh so slow and
oh so sharp. One swallow soaring overhead in spring can
be more memorable come December than the Twin Towers
coming down.

After a while, Annie started making the dinner. Even
before she said anything she'd laid three plates and set
three places. There was ten chairs at the table but her family
was up and away now. It knocked her out of kilter laying

123

the other place for Matt when she was that used to laying
for two. For her and Willie. But she done it, she laid three
places because that's what you do. She'd often thought of
the two places being reduced to one when Willie goes. If she
went first Willie would eat on the hoof sitting in the rocking
chair at the fire maybe. Aye, sitting in the rocking chair and
filling his life with work and routine. The table would never
be used again. But she never imagined three places again
at this table. Not since Robert, their youngest son, went to
London. Aye they came back and visited with their English
wives and kids and strange stories of other places. But she'd
never thought of an ordinary day and more than two at the
table. Not without the anticipation of visiting sons rippling
through her like electricity. Not a Tuesday. A grey Tuesday
with nothing remarkable about it and there she was laying
three plates.

—Will ye take a bite? she went.

Willie raised an inviting eyebrow at Matt across the
flagstones. Matt scanned the empty chairs before answering.
His eyes stopped at every chair like he was looking for
approval from the ghosts of their wandering children. He was
an eternity before saying anything.

—Aye. I will.

So he was in there for the three courser. Soup. Steak.
Apple pie. It was all served without speaking. The only sounds
were the sporadic cracking of the fire and the squeaks of
the old wood in Matt's chair. It had been a long time since it
had borne weight. Now and then Willie McGaw and his wife
exchanged polite puzzled glances. They didn't have a clue
what Matt wanted.

And he was still there an hour after the dishes had been
put back and the fire was banked up and the radio was

soothing the night in. By then Matt and Willie were back in
the chairs by the fire and Annie was polishing the vast table.
Every knot, at some time or other, she had fixed her eyes on
to get through arguments. Every grain her eyes had ran along
to the laughter round the table; her wanes leaning back,
cracking jokes and pointing at each other. The creases on
their faces is what she remembered. But now the table was a
surface of silence and edges where the lines drop off. Off into
the world of space and shadows above the hardness of the
floor. And she hoped none of her children would fall so hard
they wouldn't be able to cry for help. Or so far they'd never
be found. Or so deep nobody would hear their cries. That's all
she hoped for; the rest she left in God's hands.

Back at the fireplace Willie had poured out two drinks.

—A wee something for yourself?

Matt searched for an answer in the flames.

—Aye. I will, he went. —I will.

An hour later Matt was still there. He was still there
and blinking hard every time the clock wound and chimed
another quarter hour. Fighting sleep he was, and fighting
something else too Willie noticed, fighting something else.

Willie wasn't an impatient man. He'd learned frustration
won't bring the summer in or stop the beasts from dying. But
it was getting late and nearly time for the Good Book. He
didn't want to offend Matt by saying Protestant prayers in
front of a Catholic. He had to know what Matt wanted. He
made up his mind to ask. To give the big man an opening. It
might be money. He's never asked for that before – money.
That's what it'll be. And he's only too happy to give him some
money. Hasn't he been his neighbour all these years? Never
a bit of an argument or a dispute. Never a hint of bigotry.
Always a nod and a touch of the cap when they crossed in

opposite fields. And his brother Pat? Is he not a good God-fearing Catholic? Aye. If it's money he wants he can have it.

—Another half?

—Aye... Aye...

And while Matt was drinking the other half, Willie popped the question.

—So what'll be bringing ye here the night then Matthew?

—Ah, goes Matt, taking a sip, —Ah, now there's the thing. There's the thing right enough.

He took another sip and looked round the room. He looked round like he was looking for folks that might be listening. Or ghosts. He nodded over at the table where they had dinner hours before.

—I'm wondering – ye couldny lend me a few chairs could ye?

Willie was puzzled. So was his wife. They thought it would be something bigger.

—Chairs? No problem, said Willie.

Matt finished off what he had in his glass.

—It's our Patrick, he's passed away like. I'll be needing the chairs for the wake, he said.

The fire flared up as the midnight wind crept in under the door.

Motor Traffic Acts One And Two

When I was in my early twenties and down on my luck I stayed in this right rough scheme. Nobody was working. I got this wee Datsun for thirty quid and it ran like a sweetie. You could hardly hear the engine. I tried to get it MOT'd but there was a lot of rust on the chassis and the guy said it was a death trap. So no MOT, no insurance; no insurance, no tax.

I stole a tax disk from a car in ASDA's and used that. Flew about nice as you like. Then one day I was coming down a steep hill and the blue light of a cop car flickered across the rear view. I pulled over. One guy got out and the other one checked the registration on the radio. This was long before they had computers.

This cop, he tells me I was doing thirty-five. I looked at the Speedo even though it was broke. Said I was sorry. He starts checking the car. Don't go to the tax disc. Don't go to the tax disc. He went to the tax disc. Leaned forward, seen something he didn't like; like the registration of another car and motioned to roll the passenger window down. I leaned across but fuck it! I snibbed the door and grabbed that tax disk. He was thumping on the window but when I started eating it he ran to the driver's side. I kept him out with my feet as I chewed it to a masticated plum and swallowed. Then he done the maddest thing this cop. He burst out laughing.

Went crouching down holding onto the top of the swinging door. His mate arrived.

—What?

He couldn't talk. He just pointed at me.

—What's he laughing at? said his mate.

I shrugged.

—He ate it! blurted out this laughing cop.

—Ate what?

But his mate couldn't answer.

—The tax disc, I said.

—What did ye do that for?

I shrugged again and the laughing cop got up.

—It was for a Mercedes, he said, —I read it before he scoffed it.

And he started laughing again. Once he'd stopped he got his notebook out. And even though he was a man trying desperately to hold his laugher in, he was pretty professional.

—Name? He said biting his bottom lip.

—Derrick Riley.

—Occupation Derrick?

—Unemployed.

They looked at each other. You could tell they didn't like unemployed people. That their day was taken up with unemployed people. That unemployed people were the bane of their fuckin lives.

—Right mate will I give ye a horte or will I do ye the now?

—Just do me the now, I said.

—For?

—The works.

—Figures, said the other cop.

So they did. No tax, fraudulent tax disc, no insurance, various defective lights, three baldy tyres and an unroadworthy car. Done a bit of stand-up routine about what the charge would be for eating a tax disc; digesting the evidence. Elongating the course of investigation. Stuff like that.

They thanked me for a good laugh on this cold and wet Tuesday and made me push the car into the side of the road. Told me I couldn't drive it till I got it insured taxed and MOT'd. Said they'd be watching out for me. I hid in the new bru they were building till they were away and drove the car straight to Hanna's. Got fifteen for it. Bought a gram and two bottles of Buckie and went round to Bonzo's. Got him laughing with the story, talked about the greatest song lyrics ever and walked home stoned at two in the morning. Spent the rest of the night reading.

A year and a half after that I'd got myself a place in uni. But I was fuckin hopeless with money and done the grant in soon as I got it. When I couldn't afford the bus I stayed home and read the books. I was like a hermit and to tell you the truth I pretty much enjoyed it. I'd read straight till midday then spark up a joint and read stoned till four. Then I'd open a can if I had money for drink. It sounds crazy but coming at the work from them three angles; sober, stoned and drunk, seemed to solidify it all in my mind and when it came to exams I surprised everybody. Even myself.

Just after my second Christmas I broke into an unused garage and found a wee Peugeot. When I wiped the dust off it, it was red. I figured it would get me in and out of uni for a quid of petrol. It was me and James and Bonzo in it this day just driving about stoned. Checking the birds and listening to The Boss.

I knew it was him even though he had a helmet on. And he seen me. And he knew it was me. Even though the motorbikes were going in the opposite direction I knew they'd be coming back.

—Get rid of the dope, I said.

—Fuck off, said Bonzo and put it under his tongue.

By this time I'm a bullet down Jackson Street. But there they were, tiny in the wing mirrors; two cops, their bikes lit up like Christmas trees.

—Fuck it! I mounted the pavement banging the horn for people to get out the way. Got round left at the Whifflet lights and turned into the park. Drove right across a game of football and into the Xavierian Fathers' college.

And that's where we were sat like sailors in a submarine when two depth charges appeared over the brow, heads scanning then locking on us.

I rolled the window down. First thing he done was reach in and grab the tax disc.

—He's got a thing for these ye know, he said to James and Bonzo, —Likes to scoff them.

—It is him then? said his pal and he nodded aye.

—What have ye been up to?

—Just dossing about.

—Out the car please Derrick, said the laughing cop.

He took me aside as the other one checked the tyres and the roadworthiness.

—Do I need to ask? he said to me.

I shook my head.

—Tax?

I shook.

—Insurance?

—Nope.

—MOT?

—No.

He sighed.

—Derrick, Derrick, Derrick, he said.

The other cop came back. Shook his head and made a noise that meant death trap.

—Name.

—Ye know my name.

He wrote my name down.

—Occupation.

—Student.

The two of them looked at me.

—Place of study?

—Strathclyde University.

He said it like this as he wrote it down, —Strath-clyde University.

—Studying?

—English Literature.

That made them look at each other.

—You bullshitting? said the other cop.

—No, that's what I'm doing.

—Year? said the laughing cop, getting official again.

—Second year.

They looked at each other. The laughing cop nodded the other one away and they had a wee mumbling conference. When they came back they had a plan.

—Okay, he paused, —Name me a Shakespeare comedy.

—*As You Like It*, I said.

They confirmed that with each other.

—What's your favourite Shakespeare tragedy? asked the other one.

—*Othello*.

—Not *Macbeth*?

—I like *Macbeth*. Everybody likes *Macbeth* but what I like about *Othello* is it's got the structure of a comedy right all the way through and just when Othello sinks into his own jealousy it darkens and falls into a tragedy. I think it's the tightest tragedy, no, the tightest of all Shakespeare's plays.

The laughing cop tugged the other one away again. They spoke, looking over at me. Then they came back.

—Right Derrick, he said, —I'm only going to do you with having no tax.

—What?

But he didn't respond. He went all official.

—Derrick Riley, he said and he proceeded to charge me with having no tax.

He never mentioned the MOT, the defective lights, the wasted chassis, the insurance or the baldy tyres. It was like the conversation never happened. Gave me the receipt and the two of them jumped on their bikes, purred over the brow and out of that car park.

—What were yees talking about? said Bonzo when I got back in.

—Shakespeare.

—Shakespeare?

—Shakespeare, I said and started up the engine.

Pink River

I usually meet Tin Tin on the beach about half ten when I'm taking the collie and lurcher their last walk. He looks out to sea between his sentences. In Galloway there are long pauses between sentences. And it's nothing to pick up on the next line hours or even days later. For instance:

—Fuckin drainers it was.

—Eh?

—Drainers. The four quare fullahs. They were stealing drainers. Cast iron's worth money these days.

He was talking about four guys hanging about the harbour three days ago.

Sometimes I'd be sitting on my favourite rock watching the stars and I'd hear aye! He'd be leaning over the wall above me. He could see me but I couldn't always see him. I was from the city and my eyes weren't used to the country yet.

This Wednesday I was at a meeting in Castle Douglas. Connie took the dogs for their last walk. Floss, Tin Tin's dog, came up and then Tin Tin.

—Wuar is he the nicht then?

—Castle Douglas.

—Castle Douglas? He never told me he was gan to Castle Douglas.

When I arrived back the dogs ran up jumping and crying. Anything bigger than an hour was infinity to dogs and they thought you weren't coming back. Once they'd licked me to bits I sat beside Connie on her favourite rock. She had Bailey, the big lurcher, on her knee and Floss was trying to get Connor to play.

—Did ye do it? she said.

—Didn't get a chance, I said. —The way it went the opportunity never came up. They were all too fuckin nice.

—Maybe next week.

—Aye. I was just waiting on one of them saying something.

She chipped a stone. Connor and Floss chased it. Bailey bounded off her knee and the three of them tumbled into the water.

—Aye, said Tin Tin from the tide. It was the first I'd noticed him.

—Alright Tin Tin, I said and went over. He was looking at the moon. It was nearly full.

—Big oul moon the nicht, he said.

—Aye.

Then there was a pause. I could hear Connie talking to the dogs and doing her best to include Floss. She was like that with dogs. People she could take or leave but animals? Tin Tin was rolling a pebble in and out of the tide with his foot.

—She says ye were in Castle Douglas?

—Aye, I said and he looked at the moon. I still hadn't got used to the pauses. The moon was good but not that good.

—Never told me ye were gan to Castle Douglas, he said.

I thought I could hear Connie laughing. But if she did she covered it up by talking to dogs.

—Ye never asked Tin Tin, I said.

—No. I never, he said, as if that was okay then.

I think the tide was on the turn because it moved away from our boots and even after seven waves didn't come right back up.

—What were ye doing in Castle Douglas like?

—AA meeting, I said as if that explained everything. Of course I knew it didn't. It must've been a bit of a shock because he came back after ten seconds.

—AA?

—Aye, I said, —It's not that I'm a chronic alcoholic or anything. It's just that when I drink I'm crazy. Wreck pubs n that. Go mental.

—Aw. One of they cunts, he said. —Better no drink then.

That's all he said on the matter. He changed the subject even though it took him twenty seconds to do it.

—They got caught.

—Caught with what?

—The drainers. Gan to Stranraer. In a white van.

—Did they?

A long pause.

—Aye. Cunts that they are. Floss nearly fell down yin of the holes.

Connie was up off her rock and that was time to go. Tin Tin walked away talking. He never ever said cheerio. He walked away talking so that his voice faded. This time it was Sellafield and what we'd look like if it blew. Only forty miles due south. We'd be walking like that – he bent over – with our skin hanging off. He demonstrated and flung in a few deathly moans. Oooh! Aaah! It was clear there would be no hope for the cunts that lived closer.

In bed Connie suggested I phone Larry to come down next Wednesday. Go with me to the meeting. Maybe I'd be able to say it easier with him there.

—Say what has to be said to the fuckers and leave. You'll feel better once that's done.

—I can't ask him to travel a hundred miles to go to a meeting with me.

—He's your sponsor, she said.

Next day I phoned and explained the situation to Larry. He tried to talk me out of it. Said to be sure I wasn't acting on some big out of shape resentment. I was. But if I didn't do this I would explode. In the end he thought it would be better to go through with it. He'd arrive next Wednesday.

That was a great afternoon. The sun was blazing. We had our dinner in the garden with Larry. It was like being in Italy or something. When the meal was finished we had a laugh setting the dogs on him. Larry was terrified of dogs. You should've seen him running round the garden half laughing, half afraid. The dogs grabbing at his trouser legs.

—Get they fuckin things away from me, he was shouting.

But every time he came near me I'd grab his arms. Make it look as if he was attacking me.

—Horsey, Horsey, I'd shout to the dogs.

Don't ask me why it was horsey horsey. You'd think one word would be the same as another to a dog. But since they were pups that made them go bananas. They chased Larry round the garden. Me and Connie were doubled up laughing at the table. It was good to have Larry down and I was looking forward to the meeting.

—See if these cunts rip my jeans, Larry said. —You're fuckin paying for them.

I coaxed them over with a biscuit and Larry sat on the grass smoking a fag.

—I'm fucked, he said and lay back blowing smoke up

through the cherry trees. The smoke looked beautiful in the heat haze.

—Is the sky always blue down here? he said.

It was an hour's drive to the meeting. Larry kept commenting on the scenery. I told him wait till you see it on the way back. When the tide was high and the sun set – everything turned pink. Even the mud at the side of the river. Ripples of pink and red and ochre. He couldn't wait.

—Just be yourself the night, that's all we're asked to do, he said.

It was the usual suspects at the meeting. Some faces fell when they saw me. Whispers. The big fight we'd had six weeks previous was still on their minds. I introduced Larry and they tried to find out how long he was sober. When Larry told them thirty years you could feel the awe. He was practically a guru. I sat down but Glasgow Billy sat next to me. When I moved to another seat I seen him glancing at London Margaret.

They were on the fourth step. I won't bore you with the details except to say it's all about looking at your own faults and not other people's. London Margaret read the step and then it went round the room. Everybody said what that step meant to them. It got to Larry.

—My name's Larry and I'm an alcoholic. Aye fourth step. Nearly blew my fuckin mind that. I mean getting all that shite out my head onto paper. Cunt of a job it was. But when I done that and step five I was spiritually uplifted.

I had to admire Larry. Although he knew about my big fight six weeks ago he came and was himself. But he'd created a bad feeling in the room and I was next.

—Manny, said Margaret. When I started talking I could feel them all leaning back. And I must admit I swore more than normal. The longer I spoke the redder the faces. They were glancing at each other and shaking their heads by the time I had finished.

—Billy, Margaret said.

He wasn't next in line. I should've knew right there and then it was a set up.

—Well, he said, pushing his cup away from him like he was about to stand up. He didn't. He leaned back tapping the fingers of both hands on the table.

—Well, he said again, scanning the room. —I don't know where I'm supposed to be. But it certainly doesn't feel like an AA meeting.

He looked directly at me and said it,

—Your language is atrocious.

—What language? I said.

—That sort of language isn't acceptable at an AA meeting.

—What language is that Billy?

—Swearing.

So here it was. Larry widened his eyes at me. This was my opportunity to say what had to be said.

—I didn't come here to stop fuckin swearing. I came here to stop drinking.

—And become a better person, Billy said.

—You've got to stop swearing in order to become a better person?

—Yes.

I lifted the AA book and let it drop with a thump in the middle of the table.

—Somebody show me where it says in AA I can't swear and I'll stop it.

There was no takers for that one. I let the silence sit a moment before I spoke,

—Well, I'm not changing one fuckin syllable.

Bang! Billy slammed the table with both hands. I'd not noticed it before but he was covered in gold rings and a really expensive watch. As if he'd power-dressed for the occasion.

—Group Consciousness Meeting! Billy shouted and shot his hand up in the air.

The group copied him except for one or two allies I had. The Group Consciousness Meeting was held. The subject – should swearing be allowed? It was decided swearing would not be tolerated. I said that was fine they don't need to swear. But I'm not a member of their group so I'd fuckin swear to my heart's content.

—You leave us with no option then, said Billy, —You're barred.

—Barred from an AA meeting? Are you fuckin mental? I said.

—Please leave, he said, getting out of his chair. Maybe he was going to get physical. I don't know. Larry whispered it was time to say my bit. I asked if I could say something in my defence before I left.

—So long as you don't swear, said Billy and sat down turning his watch on his wrist.

I opened an AA book and read this section on how it was absurd for one alcoholic to judge another. We're all the exact same. Recovering drunks. Some of the punters got the gist of it and knew they were wrong. But Billy and Margaret sat bolt upright letting it wash over them.

—Finished? he asked when I closed the book

—No. I'm not, I said, —I've been coming to this meeting for a year. And I've listened to everybody in here. And d'you know something? Everybody in here swears.

I gave them all examples of how and when they swear. None of them denied it because I had their voices off to a T. Some of them had the grace to bow their heads a little. I looked directly at the instigator.

—D'you know what the problem is here Billy?

He didn't.

—What the problem is here is that I swear with a Glasgow accent. Well yees are a bunch of fuckin snobs as far as I can see. Yees can shove your meeting up your arse. I'll not be back.

—Thank God, said Billy.

—No – thank fuck, I said and left.

I was angry on the drive home but Larry calmed me. He said they were scared of me. They thought I was still that same guy that done all them crazy things. But he knew, and I knew how far I'd come. He was proud of me. I have to admit there was tears. Larry ruffled my hair and told me to stop greeting like a big lassie. When we came to Wigtown Bay the sun was going down and everything was pink.

—Fucksakes look at that! said Larry. —Pink!

I pulled over and we got out of the car. All my anger and resentment flooded into that pink river. When we got home Connie was making French toast and spinning it into the dogs' mouths.

—How did it go? she said.

Larry told Connie what happened as she made us some. Then me and Larry went down to the tide with the dogs. The moon was on the water like a silver road back to Castle Douglas. Or coming away from it. I thought Tin Tin would be out but he wasn't. We walked along talking about AA. I was telling Larry that when I first went if they didn't swear I wouldn't have went back. I'd've thought it was some kinda holy joint. He said just as we get sick from time to time – so do meetings. Meetings get sick.

They seen us before we seen them. The three Hannay Brothers. They were leaning against the harbour wall.

—Hi Manny.

—Is that you John? I said.

It was and his two brothers. I introduced them to Larry and we chatted under that big moon. John must have been sixty or seventy or eighty. It's hard to tell. His brothers were younger. He started telling this story about how his family had been fishing this sea for generations. When the brothers were young their father took them to the islands off Carrick shore. Left them with a row boat and lobster creels for three days. They slept in a wee tin hut on the island.

—What islands are they John? I said.

He pointed over to the Castle Douglas side.

—See them there? John said.

—I can't see anything.

—Och come on man – it's a full moon surely ye can see them.

I peered at the shore five miles away but couldn't see any islands.

—Where? I said.

He even stood behind me and lined up my head.

—Fucksake – there!

The brothers were trying to show Larry. But me and Larry were city boys. Or eyes were used to light.

—Sorry John, I can't see them.

He stepped back and this is what he said,

—Right. See when you're gan to Castle Douglas next Wednesday, to your meeting? Take the first cut off. The Sandgreen cut off. Then you'll see a sign for Carrick Shore.

Gan doon there and at the road end you'll see the islands. That right boys.

—Aye John.

I agreed to go and as we walked away Larry wondered how come they knew so much about my AA?

—Tin Tin, I said. And I imagined him telling the village what I'd told him on the beach that night with Connie and the dogs.

—He's an alky. Not a chronic alky. Just one of them that gans crazy when he drinks like. Wrecks the joint. Fells folks an the likes. He gans to a meeting in Castle Douglas on a Wednesday.

Larry didn't know if that was a good idea. But I felt great about it. I didn't feel like they were judging me. To them it was just a matter of fact. Like being a plumber. That was the night I felt as if I belonged to something.

Washing Machine Guy

Steve lived on top of the washing machine all winter and in the summer he lived in the pub. That was cos Maggie made chicken for the chubsters. But when the last caravan left it was time to put his bed on top of the washing machine again.

It was in the toilet with a hot towel rail next to it. I guess he liked the heat and the soothing thrum of the machine. Even a full load at 1,200 revs didn't phase him. He was one cool cat Steve. In fact that's why we called him Steve. We lost Elmo one year and Connie spent months looking for him. On one of her visits to the cat and dog home she thought Steve was Elmo. But the markings were different. Black and white, aye, but different.

Once she'd spoke to him she had to bring him home. And as I said, he was one cool cat. He sat on the couch purring like he'd been there all his days. He was so relaxed and confident we called him Steve, Steve McQueen. In the morning he was sleeping on top of the washing machine. So we bought him a new bed and he's been there ever since; every winter that is. And when the first caravans arrive in spring he's back living with Maggie.

Once when Steve was sick and we hardly knew Maggie, she arrived with a tray of roast chicken. I mean a big tray with about twenty chunks on it.

—Hi Maggie.

—This is for Steve, she said and handed it to me. Stood there wondering what to do with her empty hands. I didn't know what to say about this tray of chicken.

—It's Maggie, I shouted and Connie came out.

—How is he? said Maggie.

—Come on in, said Connie and took Maggie up to Steve. We had him locked in a room cos he had to get pills three times a day. Well, after that Maggie visited daily with chicken. Sometimes it was roast beef. I was wishing I was a cat myself.

—Hi Maggie, we'd say and up the stairs she'd go. Sometimes on her way out she'd chat but mostly she said thanks and went. But that's not the story.

The story is about the day the washing machine guy was coming. We bought this new machine. A Hotpoint washer dryer Aquarius it was. Top of the range the guy in Comet said. The latest technology. He specially pushed the self-cleaning filter. I remember clearly what he said,

—This has got a self-cleaning filter. Don't ask me how they did it, he said, —But it's inside the machine and there's no need to clean it. Does the whole thing itself.

But it started flooding after a week. This self-cleaning filter was blocking up. We phoned Hotpoint. When the washing machine guy came he said the filter was blocked.

—I thought it was self-cleaning?

—It is. But it's blocked, he said.

I let that hang a moment then screwed my eyes up. —But if it's self-cleaning it shouldn't block – am I right?

—Technically yes… but…

—So it's not self-cleaning. This self-cleaning filter isn't actually self-cleaning?

—It's blocked.

—I know it's blocked, I told your office it was blocked, what I want to know is why it's blocked – seeing as how it's a self-cleaning filter.

—It's blocked.

—Look, I said, —is it self-cleaning or not?

—I can't comment on that.

By then the machine had finished its test cycle and he clicked his case shut. Got me to sign a form and left.

It flooded again the next day. I could've fixed it but I figured why should I if I paid four-fifty for it? And anyway this filter; you could only get at it through the back of the machine. And that would null and void the guarantee. So we called them again. They said yes the engineer had already been out. But I said no that was yesterday and asked them all about the self-cleaning filter that doesn't. But I got avoidance. I didn't even speak to the washing machine guy when he came out. I signed the form and off he went.

By the fifth time we were starting to get frustrated. I pressured him about a self-cleaning filter that didn't self-clean but this washing machine guy wouldn't be quoted on anything.

So Connie called Comet head office. She had a big fight, quoting the Sale of Goods Act and all this legal stuff. Comet said they'd send their engineer and if he found a fault he'd give us a number, a code, to get our machine replaced.

But he came on a bad day. Planning had just been approved on a building with windows staring into every corner of our house. We were up early watching the building start. The street was rattling with lorries and cars and that's when the door went. I got my story ready for this new

145

washing machine guy but it wasn't him. It was Maggie. And she was crying.

—It's Steve, she said. —He's not moving.

Connie told me to wait for the Comet guy and went out through the builders and down to the pub.

When the door opened it was Connie with Steve flopped in her arms. She had to go to the vet. I clapped Steve and he responded but you could tell there was something far wrong. Out at the car, with the building racket rising I clapped him again and this time you could see him disappear. I looked at Connie and she looked at me. She swung the car door out with her knee. One of the builders whistled and I looked up. But it wasn't the time for trouble. Connie drove away and I heard this builder shouting something like what the fuck're you staring at as I closed the door.

I sat with my mind flitting between the machine and the building and Steve. The door went. It was Comet this time.

—Comet, he said.

—Oh the washing machine, I said, as if I'd forgot it.

But I had to open the double doors and I don't think he liked that. He avoided all eye contact as he squeezed in and right there I knew there was no code coming out of him.

—It's up there, I said. And when he was tinkering about I asked if he wanted a cup tea. Or coffee.

—No thanks, he said.

I made some coffee and stood thinking about Steve. How Connie was going to take it. I could hear the washing machine guy huffing and puffing in the hall. The machine scraping about and a ratchet. When I was sure he was into the filter I went out.

—The filter's not cleaning, I said.

—No wonder. It's filled with hair.

—But it's supposed to be self-cleaning, I said.

—To a point.

—To a point?

—It's blocked, he said and held out a wad of hair for me to see. I got the feeling I was supposed to be disgusted.

I told him that's what I said on the phone. That the filter was blocked. I knew the filter was blocked, any idiot would know the filter was blocked. What I wanted to know is why they'd put a self-cleaning filter that didn't self clean inside a machine where nobody could get at it. When I finished ranting he was staring at me. Here was man that doesn't like anybody else knowing about washing machines.

—It's blocked, he said, and this time he said it with finality.

—Jesus. I know it's blocked. But it shouldn't be blocked should it? It's self-cleaning!

He stared at me. I could see he fancied his chances with me. But he was one of them fat bastards that mistake size for muscle.

—There's excessive hair in the filter. That's why it's flooding.

—Aye it's filled with hair cos it's not cleaning, I said, —so I want it replaced.

—I can only replace it if it's got a fault, he said.

—It has got a fault it's got a self-cleaning filter that doesn't clean.

—You've got dogs.

—Aye, I said, —But I don't put them in the fucking washing machine.

—I'd appreciate it if you didn't swear Mister Brennan.

—And I'd appreciate it if you took that machine to fuck out of here and brung me another one, and I went face to face to say this: —With a filter on the outside!

—I'll have to call my boss.

He crushed past me and I had this sudden urge to punch him. He went out into his van and I seen him criticising me on his mobile. When he came back he said his boss would call me.

—When?

—When he's got time.

—When will that be?

—I don't know.

—Well, will it in the next five minutes,

—I don't know.

—The next hour?

—I don't know.

—Well – will it be days or weeks?

—When he's got time.

I watched him putting the machine back together.

—So are ye giving me the code?

—My boss is going to call you.

—So you're not giving me the code?

—My boss is going to call you.

He set up a test and I went into the kitchen. That's when Connie came back with Steve in her arms. Dead. She was crying. She came into the kitchen and asked me what happened. When I told her she handed me Steve and went to see the guy. He was watching the tub fill up with clear water.

—So you're not changing it?

—My boss is going to call you.

—Are ye changing it or are ye not?

—It was full of dog hair.

—Yes, we've got dogs, she said.

He shrugged and said that's why it was blocked. It wasn't a fault it was dog hair. Excessive dog hair.

148

—Are you saying I've got a dirty house?

—Whatever! he said and my blood surged.

—It shouldn't be blocked with hair. It should be getting rid of every hair as it comes in if it's a self-cleaning-filter, she said.

—It's not designed to deal with excessive hair.

—How much hair is it designed to deal with?

—Eh?

—A handful. Ten? Twenty. Many?

—Not dog hair.

—So why doesn't it say – this machine is not designed to deal with dog hair? Do not buy this machine if you've got dogs?

—I'm only the engineer.

—There's something wrong with that machine and you're covering it up aren't ye?

—We've had no other complaints.

—A quarter of Britaln's got dogs, Connie said. —There must be a fair number of them have this exact machine, are you telling me you've not had any complaints from them?

—None.

—Okay, said Connie. —If you've had no complaints from people with dogs then there must be something wrong with this specific machine.

—Eh? he said and she repeated it but I don't think his brain was set up for that kind of logic so he said whatever again. And he kept saying whatever. And every time he said it my rage rose. And the hammering outside was tinging in my ears. I made to put Steve on the worktop. But I couldn't do that. I couldn't put him on the worktop. The only place that seemed right was his bed. And that was on top of the washing machine. This dead cat, Steve, it was the only thing stopping me from going out there and laying into the washing machine guy. My temper was on spin cycle as I hiked from place to place in that kitchen with a dead cat in my arms. By then Connie was shouting.

—Hey, here's some news for ye. —A fucking revelation, she said, —Human beings have got hair too! she said, —Not unless that machine's only for baldy bastards.

—Whatever.

—If you say whatever one more time I'll stick your big meaty head in that machine, Connie shouted.

I don't know why but I laughed at that. I think it was big meaty head. So there was me leaning against the cooker sniggering, two different kinds of tears coming down my face, my ears ringing and a dead cat in my arms. So when he said whatever again I burst out laughing. Loud and clear it was.

And he left. He started his car and manoeuvred through piles of bricks and wood and scaffolding stuff. Connie came into the kitchen and burst out crying. We held onto each other with Steve between us.

We put him in his bed on top of the washing machine. He felt alive. He looked alive. His eyes were wide open and you thought he was looking right back. Connie said to leave it till we were sure.

—Till we're absolutely sure, she said.

We tucked him in and took a couple of photos. He was so beautiful with his eyes open. Even though there was no washing Connie turned the machine on for Steve's last snooze. As it thrummed away she called Hotpoint to complain. What she got from them was another load of abuse. And they told her our guarantee was null and void because we'd allowed a Comet engineer to open the machine. Clang clang went the scaffolders.

When the full wash was over rigor mortis had set in. We went for Maggie and buried Steve in the garden and threw in a few clematis. There's more to life than leaking washing machines but that day it sure didn't seem like it.

Holy Heater

By the time we could see the hills, snow had started to fall.
Danny said it was hard to believe ten years had passed since
Carpet John first took him. He'd smashed his house up for
the umpteenth time and his wife had went back to her
maw's with the kids. Kids never out of hospital with mystery
illnesses.

Ten years on they were healthy as plums and all at
university. Danny had his own business. His wife was happy.
All that was left of his drinking days was bad memories and
a lack of social etiquette. He would've insulted folks more
frequently if he wasn't for his charm. But me? I loved him all
the more for it.

—I hope the daffodils are up, Danny said to me. —That's
what I remember. The daffodils.

When we got to the stone arch the daffs were standing to
attention. Hi Danny – long time no see. Easter last year was
it? And the year before, and the year before… They leaned
in as we approached and out in the rear view mirror, flicking
snowdust. The guest house was a fairy tale; snow on the roof
and turrets. Winding Salvation Armies of daffodils converging
from every path. We were the first car since the snow and it
was good gliding over that world of white. The lights were
on and people were coming to the windows. It was three and

time for tea so we left the bags till later. The Guest Master was at the big oak door to welcome us.

—Danny, how are you? he said.

Danny introduced me. I love the way monks shake your hand. They take it gently. As they say your name they cradle your hand with both hands. They look you in the eye. But it doesn't make you paranoid. It calms you down.

—These guys are really holy, Danny, I said, —Ye can feel it emanating from them.

Danny just gave me a look and by the end of our visit I knew what that look meant.

The stone hallway filled with cups rattling and the murmur of voices. Tea and biscuits. In the dining hall there was about thirty people. About half of them were AA punters but I only knew three of them. Danny got a cheer when he walked in. Danny this and Danny that they were going. Everybody loved Danny.

We got our tea and listened to complaints about the cold nights. Poundstretchers Maggie from the Gorbals Friday Night coughed and said they were queuing to do the dishes cos of the hot water. There was twelve AA punters so we had a meeting in one of the rooms at seven. Maggie shared and Bear Hug Bob chaired. When it was finished we all went to bed spiritually charged.

Me and Danny humped our bags up to St Patrick's at the very top of the building. Danny called the top floor Saint Siberia. The higher we went the colder it got. I could see fog in the landing.

—Look Danny, Fog! I said.

But Danny told me not to be daft. Stop havering. It's probably just the DTs still wearing off. But there was mist creeping at us from the end of the corridor. It was giving me the fear so Danny went to investigate. One of the old windows was stuck open. He said it was stuck open last year an all. There wasn't much money and the monks relied on people with tools and time. But they concentrated on the first floor rooms for women or married couples.

Our room on Saint Siberia was two wooden beds, two wardrobes like your granny had, and two writing desks.

—People get a lot off their chest here, Danny said. — Writing alone in your room is recommended.

—Writing about what?

—Your life, he said and went to the window.

The wind was coming in the window frame so Danny stuffed paper towels in the cracks. We said The Third Step prayer together before we got into our beds. He started and I joined in. I've got to say I felt like a right dick saying it:

—God I offer myself to thee to build with me and to do with me as thou wilt. Relieve me of the bondage of self, that I may better do thy will. Take away my difficulties that victory over them may bear witness to them I would help of thy power, Thy love and Thy way of life. May I do Thy will always.

I fell asleep repeating the words in my head. A deep deep sleep it was. But I was woke up an hour later by Danny in the pitch black.

—Michael? Michael are ye wakened?

—Well, I am now.

—I'm freezing.

That's when I noticed so was I. I suggested we put our clothes back on. We did and I fell asleep in seconds. But Danny woke me up again.

—Michael are ye wakened?

—No!

—I'm still freezing.

—So am I.

Danny wanted me to go into his bed. Wrap round each other. Keep warm.

—What are you? Some kinda poof?

—Maybe, he said and laughed, —C'mon see.

Danny lit a match and I went over. All this talk about cold was making me even colder anyway. I dragged all my blankets over. But, just in case he was a poof I made Danny wrap a blanket round himself and I wrapped up in one.

—You'd need to be Houdini the Magic Poof to get near me, I said.

And he laughed too loud for that building. As the match burned out we were two sausage rolls. We pulled the pile of covers over and lay spooned like a married couple. We laughed and joked about it a bit. I don't know who fell asleep first.

When I woke I was blinded by white. The whole room was lit up like the Holy Spirit. There was frost ferns all over the window. I hadn't seen that since central heating. Danny woke and said it was the coldest night he's ever spent in the monastery. He looked at the ferns.

—Aw look at that, he said, —Is that not beautiful?

At eight o'clock mass everybody looked brisk and chilly. Except Poundstretchers Maggie. All through the mass she couldn't stop coughing and snottering and shivering. I whispered to Danny and you could see he was concerned. We grabbed her after mass.

—Been on the Buckfast? said Danny.

—I wish I was, she said. —I'm freezing.

—We'd to go into bed thegether, Danny said.

—Oh aye – kinky. Hey! Live and let live, she said, putting her palms in the air to absolve us of all poofery.

—Why don't ye slip in between us the night, said Danny.

—Oh aye, the monks'll love that will they not?

The breakfast bell was going and she came to our table. As we tucked into the porridge Danny overheard a married couple telling a priest on retreat the Guest Master had put a heater in their room.

—It certainly isn't warm Father, but it takes the bite out of the air.

The priest praised the lord that he had asked for a fire too and they carried on with the type of conversation you get with priests.

—The monk's got heaters, Danny whispered to Maggie, in case he caused a landslide for heaters, —Go'n ask him for one!

—I can't just walk up and ask for a heater.

—They've got one, said Danny and leaned across, —Hey! Have youse got a heater in your room?

—Yes, was all they said and returned to their conversation. Asking about a heater was like inquiring into her sex life. The woman looked at the ceiling for the priest's benefit. Danny seen her.

—Snobby cow, he said, too loud. The woman pretended not to hear it.

As me and Danny demolished every morsel of food on the table Danny persuaded Maggie to ask the Guest Master. She's a woman. She shouldn't be up in Saint Siberia anyway. She should be down in one of the good rooms. Or at least have a heater. If he's giving heaters to couples in the good rooms then he's surely going to give one to a woman on her own up in Frostville!

She was persuaded. Up she went and we watched her talking to the monk. But you could see there was no heater

157

coming out of him. His shoulders were up and his palms were out. Crucifying himself on the lack of a heater. He patted Poundstretchers Maggie on the back. Twice. Pat pat – there there. He'd given them all out. He was sorry that he didn't have a heater to give her. Maggie came back.

—He's not got one. He's gave them all out.

At least her shivering had stopped. And she jumped and smiled when Danny felt her arse to cheer her up.

—See you, she whispered. —This is a bliddy monastery!

She went off with a smile on her face. More cos we'd tried to help her than Danny feeling her arse. Although Danny swore blind it was the arse.

Me and him went into the hills. The skies were clear blue and our breath was steam. But there was enough sun to keep the right side of chilled. Danny had snaffled a couple of caramel logs out the kitchen and we ate them beside a silver loch. He made a red and gold boat from the wrappers and set it free on that loch. We watched till it was just an intermittent glint in the sun.

—That's what AA does Michael, he said, —Sets ye free.

He talked about morality. And when he did he was lucid and clear. I suppose it was my own snobbery that made me amazed that he could talk about morality. And make plenty sense. He dissected incidents in my life step by step. Showed me how my choices brought me trouble. Trouble I had blamed on others my whole life. Trouble I blamed on bad luck. Trouble I blamed on somebody up there. Somebody up there who hated me. But Danny said it was impossible for somebody up there to hate me. He even said it was impossible to hate yourself.

—I don't believe that Danny, I said. —I hated myself when I was drinking. I still hate myself.

—Ye love yourself.

—No – I don't.

—Aye, ye do, he said, without aggression.

—No.

And he told me that even when he was stuck in the throes of alcoholism he always wished things were better. I had to agree there. I knew exactly what he meant. Even now he's trying to get a better home, a better relationship with his wife and kids. Better friendships. That's cos he loves himself. He told me I was in this monastery cos I wanted better things for myself. I looked out over the water but I wasn't at peace. I had this burning desire to be right. To have the last word. I searched for a way to prove him wrong.

Then

I got it.

I found a situation where I didn't love myself but, so as not to alert him, I started what sounded like a conversation.

—Did ye ever feel shame guilt and remorse Danny?

—Every time I sobered up.

—Were ye ever in despair with the drink?

—A lot of times.

—No, but real deep despair.

—A lot of times.

—Were ye ever suicidal?

He showed me his wrists. I'd never noticed the longways gouges up his forearms. He told me of another time when he took pills. And when he was younger he jumped off a railway bridge. Broke both legs and a rack of ribs. And when he got out of hospital he went straight back and jumped again. I had him. I had the bastard now. I sprung it.

—Ye couldn't've loved yourself much then Danny.

—Eh?

—You said we love ourselves all the time. Never stop loving ourselves.

—Aye?

—Jumping off a railway bridge – twice! – doesn't sound like love to me. Fuckin ripping your wrists, gobbling up paracetamol – doesn't sound like love at all that!!!

—Ah! But it is, he said and he didn't even flinch.

—How d'you make that out?

—'Cos, bonehead, life was so unbearable I wanted to bring about an end to my suffering. If I hated myself I'd've kept on suffering.

That day was a turning point in my sobriety. I started to admire Danny all the more. His grip on morality. We walked back in silence taking in the cold sunset. I felt strangely at peace. And another thing; I was dying for a chance to make a moral decision. To impress Danny by making the right choice. That chance wasn't long in coming.

The top layer of snow had turned to ice and was crunching under our feet. You could hear us coming for miles as we marched along in unison singing Onward Christian Soldiers but not really meaning it. We got back in time for the last meal at five o'clock.

Me and Danny and Maggie sat at a table. It had been set for five and when they served the steak pie and chips they put five portions out. Me and Danny ate the other two steak pies. Gave Maggie the extra two sweets. She'd be needing the blood sugar to keep warm. That's when I heard the rumbling. So did Danny. We turned and coming up the driveway bursting through the crust of ice was this Jaguar. It was red and it moved as if any minute it would crash through into the abyss. We could make out two people sitting upright.

The Guest Master brought them in with clouds of cold and

it was obvious he knew them. A few diners waved the small polite waves you see in classical concerts and churches. The Guest Master pointed at our table and down they came. She was tall and blonde over grey. Sharp features and about fifty with a good figure still. Overdressed in fact for a retreat in a monastery. In this sexually rarefied atmosphere you couldn't help but notice her legs. As Danny said – You'd shag her if you'd nothing else to do. Her husband was smaller, more shrunk into himself and definitely not the boss. He managed to make an expensive suit look shabby. She removed her glove and stuck her hand in my face.

—Bernadette O'Rourke, she said.

I don't know if she wanted me to kiss it or shake it. I shook it anyway and she done the same with Danny and Maggie. She introduced Patrick her husband before they sat down.

—He's a solicitor.

I got the feeling we weren't as overawed as she expected. She asked Danny what he was and when he said a right fuckin alky me and Maggie laughed. It was the first I'd seen anger with a smile. She asked where the other two portions of steak pie were. We shrugged.

—Father said there were two places set for us at this table. Two steak pies.

—We scoffed them, said Danny.

—Pardon? Whether Danny knew that Pardon was Bernadette's version of you fuckin what? I don't know. But he leaned over and shouted in her face.

—We scoffed them. Then me and him (me) and she (Maggie) scoffed your sweets.

—You ate our meals? Well really. We've been travelling for three hours I'll have you know.

—And that's why you're late. And that's why you've got

no grub, he said, leaning back and slapping belly, —If you're not fast you're last missus!

She scraped her chair out and clacked across to the Guest Master, telling him and pointing over. It was an outrage for both of them. The monk told her he'd get the cook to prepare something else. Something even better than steak pie. As she complained Danny leaned over to her husband. And this is exactly what he said:

—You better nip out and get her a curry mate or you'll not be getting your hole the night!

—I beg your pardon!!?

—Better get down the Chinkee's quick fast and get her a chicken curry and fried rice or the knickers'll be staying up the night.

If he'd had any dinner the solicitor would've choked on it. Maggie got up and went into the hall. I could hear her laughter exploding, the main door opening and closing. Then she appeared under the window doubled up against the snow. She'd stop laughing then something would make her look up to me and Danny and she'd double up again. Folded into her own cloud. Bernadette returned with an air of triumph.

—The chef is cooking us something special, she said to Patrick but really to us.

Patrick decided not to mention what Danny said. You could tell he was used to keeping the peace. Another grey hair appeared on his head. The Guest Master came to the table and, looking at me and Danny, asked the O'Rourkes if everything else was all right. She happened to mention how cold it was in the building. Especially with the air conditioned heating they have in the Jaguar. The Guest Master said he'd run up and pop a heater in their room. Me and Danny looked at each other. I stood up but Bernadette had a word for us as we left.

—In future ask before you devour other people's food.

—I could hardly ask if ye weren't here could I, blondie! said Danny. For a minute I thought he was going to feel her arse.

Later, when the Guest Master was drinking coffee with the O'Rourkes, I jooked up to the good rooms. When I opened the door the heat hit me. There it was: three red bars glowing in the dark. I pulled the plug out, got it by the handle and sprinted up the spiral staircase to Saint Siberia. Put it in Maggie's room and turned it on. Full blast. Boy was she in for a surprise tonight.

It was a right cold night. Colder than the first one. Me and Danny even had the mattress from my bed flung over us. The next morning at eight o' clock mass everybody was shaking off the effects. There were runny noses. Blue hands. Crusty hair. Hastily flung on clothes. Slept in clothes. And in the front row Bernadette and Patrick were blue and shivering. Unless they'd been on the Buckie all night, me and Danny were guessing they had a bad night of it. In the middle of this Arctic tundra was Poundstretchers Maggie. Standing like a little contented penguin. All fluffy and warm and filled with God's love. Her clothes ironed. She'd had a good shower and looked like a woman living in the Ritz.

After mass Maggie came running up and thanked us for the heater. We were great boys finding a heater for her. We told her to keep her voice down.

—Shht Maggie, said Danny. —Or I'll feel your arse.

At breakfast, Bernadette and Patrick sat with their backs to us. Shivering. Holding their cups with both hands. The Guest Master smiled and asked if they'd had a pleasant night.

163

It was the worst night she'd spent in years. And as politely as she could she ripped into the Guest Master about to the heater he promised.

—I put it in last night.

—Eh – you did not.

—I did. Immediately after I said I would.

Bernadette couldn't call a man of the cloth a liar.

—It wasn't there when we went to bed then Father, she said.

That was the moment Maggie's head fell and she whispered through her hair.

—Tell me yees didn't.

—Didn't what? said Danny. —Steal their heater and put it in your room?

—Well, I whispered. —Who does that monk think he is telling you there's no heaters and as soon as he hears a posh accent it's oh here! Three bars.

But Maggie wasn't in a mood for ethics. She shot up to her room. Unplugged the heater and stashed it in some corner cupboard in an unused room in Saint Siberia. It wasn't found till summer. She rushed back down and walked in slow so as not to arouse suspicion. The Guest Master was on his feet banging a cup off the table. He got everybody's attention. Maggie sat down drawing me and Danny a look.

—A reading, said the Guest Master. And he read from the bible all the time staring at me and Danny.

—The thief cometh not, but for to steal, and to kill, and to destroy: I am come that they might have life, and that they might have it more abundantly.

Then he launched into his attack.

—Someone, sometime last night, entered a guest's room and stole.

164

—Oh! said everybody. Me and Danny too.

—They removed a heater from a room.

—Oh! said the dining room.

But not as loud as the first time. Most of them could understand stealing a heater. There's theft and there's theft.

—I'm giving those responsible an opportunity to own up.

Me and Danny scanned the place waiting for the culprits to stand. But most people were looking at us. Especially Bernadette and Patrick.

—Fine, said the Guest Master. —If I find out who it was they will be banned from this establishment for life.

Everybody agreed with that. But I thought it was a bit harsh for a first offence. Banned for life. Where was his Christian charity? I wanted to stand up and tell everybody what had happened. To let them see it was the monk in the wrong. But Danny could see it in my eyes. He put his hand on mine and said.

—Leave it. Ye done the right thing.

And he winked.

Immigrants

We cashed our Giros and bought one way tickets to Rotterdam via Hull. The size of the ship frightened me. Rising up black and hard from the sea and shimmering with frost above the waterline. And Hull? Brown. That's what Hull is. Brown and wet. Except where dirty ice gathered at the edge of the river.

We dumped our cases and went to the duty free. There was these gigantic bottles of Grouse that came up to your waist and they were only twenty quid. How could you pass a bargain like that? We figured we could afford one and maybe hitch hike down to the ICI.

—What's a thousand miles? John said, —We could live on bread and milk. Sleep in bus shelters and stuff.

We got the bottle and made a pact to open it a hundred miles from the ICI. You got a dinner on the boat and a breakfast coming into Rotterdam. Free. You could go round as many times as you wanted. We were like two beached whales when we were finished. That's when John came up with one of his ideas. He was good at ideas, John. Seeing as how we'd only thirty quid left we could take a few loaves and some cold meat to keep us going till we got to the ICI.

—Great, I said, —Everything's looking rosy now John.

We talked about the mega bucks we'd make at the ICI.

Save a hundred and fifty, maybe two hundred a week. Set up our own business when we came home. Window cleaning maybe? A van. Aluminium ladders. Get all the equipment for cleaning shop windows. Maybe get the ASDA contract? We could start other people. We could end up millionaires! John suggested a pint to wash the dinner down. I reminded him of the pact not to drink till we were near the ICI.

—What harm's one beer going to do? he said.

We woke up with our faces stuck to the carpet. The giant bottle of Grouse was half empty. I had some hangover. And so did John cos he was already swigging. He handed it over and I glugged a curer down. Breakfast was already being served.

—Come on, he says. —Get a couple of carrier bags.

When I stood up the whole world was jelly and Rotterdam was closing in. I felt if you leaned against the steel walls they'd bend. We filled two duty free bags with bread meat cheese apples bananas and wee tubs of butter. One of the crew came over and asked for money in foreign. But we told him get to fuck.

It was dawn when we got to the centre of Rotterdam. Everybody was skidding on ice. Holland smelled different. All I can remember is orange. Orange buses. Orange buildings. Orange trams. And red and maybe yellow. The whole place looked like something out a comic. Bright and shiny. Clean as a pin. Rotterdam looked like a toy town.

We left the bags and the half finished giant bottle of Grouse in the left luggage and wandered the streets. John asked these four Bob Marleys digging the road if there was any work. They passed their joint to us.

—No work here, they said, —You English?

—Are we fuck! John said, —We're Scottish.

The Three Musketeers was the place to find work. That's
where all the English went. Things were looking up. John
thought we might be able to get a job in Rotterdam and put
a few quid by to get us down to the ICI.

—Fuck we might even buy an old car and drive down, he
said.

The Three Musketeers was small and dark. Turns out the
guys were mostly from Bristol. We bought a round and that
was us down to forty guilders. John stuck that down his
sock for emergencies then asked if there's any jobs going
anywhere. But these guys were all looking for work.

—And you'll find a lot boozing in here all day ya lazy
English bastards, I said.

It went quiet and then this massive guy laughed. Then
they all laughed. And he ordered us drinks from the bird
behind the bar. We were soon all drunk and the crack was
good. Turns out there was no work in Holland and not a lot
in Germany either. But they kept buying drink and the more
we drank the less important work became. These guys liked
my crack. I told them about sellotaping my granny's budgie
to its perch when it died and they fell about laughing. They
couldn't stop. The big guy stopped long enough to order
more drinks.

—Wouldn't mind a shag at that thing, I said about the
bird behind the bar.

—D'you like her mate?

—What, tits like that and an arse like two boiled eggs in
a hankie? The place went quiet. Only sound was the glasses
filling. Then your man laughed again.

—That's my bird, he said and all his men join in the
laughing.

Later we're at a table and Bristol is asking what we're

going to do with no money and no work.

—We're going down to Germany to the ICI job.

But Bristol's got an idea. How we can make a fortune and quick. There's this jeweller and he locks up every night at six. Goes through a narrow alley to his car. Carries the day's takings. All we need to do is knock him out, take the money, give Bristol ten percent and get to fuck to Germany before the cops start nosing about.

—There's about ten grand in his bag, he said.

Me and John rationalised it. I mean he's rich. What's a bump on the head to a rich guy? The Tories in Scotland were making us pay for being poor. It's poetic justice that we should rob a jeweller. Out loud it sounded great. It was right. Christ! It sounded like a crusade the way we were going on.

Next thing we're in a wee yellow Ford Escort bombing through the city. There's trams and people going home from work. All wrapped up. We pulled over near the shop.

—Ten minutes, said Bristol.

Through the glass I could see a shadow moving.

—That's him tidying up, Bristol says, —Not long now.

So we wait, looking across slant ways at that shop. And the tension builds. There's no talking and you can taste the adrenaline on the back of your tongue. Then Bristol drops this into the silence,

—He's got a gun, so you'll have to hit him right away. Knock him out.

He's got a gun. That keeps going through my head. He's got a gun. I looked at John. We gave each other the nod and the two back doors opened like wings.

—This way, John shouts and we're off into a busy street. I can't remember if Bristol shouted but I suppose he must have. Next thing John's on a moving tram giving me a hand on. We slump into a couple of chairs. We're quiet at first and then we laugh. There's no fares on the trams there. They trust you to buy a ticket. That's when John had another idea. Go to the station and jump a train into Germany.

When we met up with that giant bottle of Grouse our eyes lit up. All that robbery gave me a right drouth. We started swigging.

—A gun, John? What did they not tell us about the gun for? John says he knew it was too good to be true. If all you had to do was clunk the jeweller over the head why had Bristol and his mates not done it before? It should have been obvious.

—This is a gun country. And we'd better get used to that, says John.

The more me and him drank the less scary the gun seemed. And after an hour we were toying with the idea of hanging about another night and having a go at the Jeweller ourselves. But we decided it was too long to wait.

—Best to head into Germany, John says.

In the station people were looking at us. We must've been a sad sorry sight with our carrier bags of food, two battered old cases and the big bottle of Grouse. There was a train to Köln. I was sure that was in Germany. So was John. We decided that was our train.

It was packed. Me and John got an aisle seat each facing each other. Everybody had suits and briefcases. This was a long distance train but the Dutch used it to commute to Utrecht.

The woman next to me had a fur coat. She leaned away from me. I suppose we must have smelt cos we'd been on the road a wee while now. Once the train got going John got the giant bottle out. When he swung it up I had to lean back.

The bottom went past my face like a golden moon with the colour draining out. Everybody was muttering in Dutch. Look at the state of these two cunts probably. John passed me the bottle and it was his turn to see the golden moon rising.

—D'you know if this train goes anywhere near the ICI? says John to the guy beside him.

The Guy hugs his briefcase and looks out the window. But the train goes into a tunnel and my reflection is looking right back at him. I think he settled on the forehead of the woman who was leaning away from me. John thought we might as well make good use of the time. He dipped into one of the carrier bags and handed me some slices of bread that had started to curl. Next he handed me a pile of squelchy gammon. It was sweating and the smell hit the woman. She covered her nose with a hanky. Everybody was squinting at us.

I didn't want to but there was no other option. In the middle of the window was a wee fold down flap. About the perfect size of two slices of bread. I leaned over and sat the pile of bread down. I put the gammon on my knee and John opened a few wee tubs of butter.

—Did ye get a knife? I says. But he never got a fuckin knife. Did I think he's got to remember everything? He thought I got the knife. I asked him if he thought there would be any knifes on the train.

—Just use your finger, he says.

—My finger!?

I didn't want to embarrass myself. But what else could I do? You should have seen the faces as I scooped the butter out and spread it on the bread. Lucky, in the heat of the train, it melted into the bread. My elbow was digging into the woman every time I leaned over. Then a bit of butter

172

fell on her coat. She tutted to the passengers and away she went. The last I saw she was getting into another seat the far end of the carriage. The man next to John done the same. Everything worked out well. With the extra space we got tore in. Finished in jig time. Sat there eating a few and slugging the Grouse. Watching the white world stream past. All the canals were froze over.

We packed the sandwiches tight in the bags to keep them fresh. John dozed off and I looked out over the Dutch countryside. I kept remembering the story of the wee boy that stuck his finger in the dyke. Then his hand. Then his leg. And finally his whole body. He saved Holland from drowning. I liked that wee boy. Always wanted to be like him. Some kind of hero. But there wasn't much call for heroes where we came from. I fell asleep dreaming about this wall surrounding an infinite expanse of dark water. And you could tell that underneath was the houses and rooms and skeletons of everybody that perished. They perished because the boy was drunk. I was the boy. And people were pointing at me. Accusing me. Digging their fingers in to my shoulder. And a voice. In Dutch.

—Hello! Hello!

I opened my eyes and it was the Ticket Man.

—Tickets, he says.

—No.

—Where you go?

—Köln.

He looked up a wee book and calculated. I couldn't understand him but you could see it was a big number by his face. And you could see he thought it was a number we didn't have. All we had was the forty guilders down John's sock. I had to do something.

—John!

But John was solid gone. The Ticket Man said the big number again. I had no choice.

—We don't want any tickets.

—No. You not understand, you must buy ticket for journey.

—I know we must buy ticket for journey but we don't want any.

The carriage was listening. Even the wheels seemed to be turning in mid air. He asked me again.

—You must have ticket. Come on. He shook John. —Come on.

John woke blinking. I told him what was happening and he stood up. He grabbed the Ticket Man.

—Look pal we don't want any tickets now fuck off!

John pushed him. He staggered back a few steps before turning and marching away. The whole train was disgusted. The passengers shrunk behind papers. Into magazines. I was worried but John calmed me. Said the train was going into Germany. The Ticket Man's Dutch.

—What's that got to do with it John? I said, —I don't understand what that's got to do with it?

—He'll probably get off at the border and another Ticket Man'll come on. Most of these people'll be getting off at Utrecht. So they won't be able to grass us up.

He made a lot of sense. I settled in. We'd been on the train a wee while now so Utrecht must be getting closer. And closer and closer and closer and closer and closer and closer and closer

And closer.

I came out of my doze cos the train was slowing down.

—John! Utrecht! I said. But something wasn't right. Bags

and briefcases were still on racks and papers still spread out like sails powering them home to slippers, meals and comfy chairs.

—Toilet, John said, —Quick!

We got the carrier bags, our cases and the Grouse and headed to a toilet three carriages up. John got in first and I piled the cases on him. I squeezed in and locked the door. It was hard taking slugs of the Grouse in that confined space. You had to get it right up cos it was nearly finished now. The food was crushed too. The train slowed and slowed. I said to John it was crazy that twenty-four hours ago we were in the post office cashing our Giros and now we're stuffed into a bog on a train halfway between Rotterdam and fuckin Utrecht. He laughed first and then I followed. I didn't know why we were laughing. I tried to swing the giant Grouse but John was leant forwards. Then the door went.

Bang bang bang. We held our breath.

—Is there anyone in there? This voice shouted with a Dutch accent. When he knocked again John couldn't resist it.

—Nobody here but us chickens! He shouted and sent us into hysterics again.

—Let us in.

—Not by the hair on my chinny chin chin, I said.

They started kicking the door. The lock broke and the door kept hitting my leg but the more I shouted the more they kicked. John stuck a hand out to get them to stop but he whipped it back in and it was bleeding. They must've banged it with a truncheon.

—Stop! He shouted. —Stop, we're coming out. We're coming out.

The kicking stopped and I stood up and squeezed out, then John. All these cops were there with leather jackets and guns. Pointing at us.

—John, guns.

The Transport Police dragged us off the train. It was
a petrochemical plant lit up like the middle of Christmas.
When they were taking us away I kept shouting about
our sandwiches and the Grouse. But they didn't care. John
was going mental about his case. Kept shouting if there's
anything missing he was going to sue them. Next thing we
were in Utrecht railway station. They took John away.

—Tell them nothing, he was shouting.

I was wondering what not to tell them cos we'd not done
anything. Just tried to jump a train. I got flung in a room
with a giant mirror. Then it was quiet. The kind of quiet that
eventually makes you think. Then I thought I could hear
voices. Somebody shouting. Sometimes when the drink's
wearing off I hear the voices. But I can never make out what
they're saying. I stared at my reflection, concentrated to take
my mind off it. But the more I stared the louder the voices
got. I covered my ears and stared till I didn't recognise myself.
Then I kept staring till I looked like a complete stranger. I
thought of that guy in the mirror thinking about cashing
his Giro to go to Germany and make a fortune. Certain he'd
drive home in a big Merc. His pal John said they were cheaper
in Germany. If they worked long enough they'd be able to
get one. John's was going to be white. The man in the mirror
fancied a red one. In his country he could only dream about
owning a Merc. But in Germany it could be a reality.

Two cops came in and said they were going to fine us. I
told them I had no money. But they kept asking for cash to
pay the fine. I told them I didn't have any. That we bought
the tickets with our Giros. I tried to explain what Giros were
but I don't think they got it. They said if we didn't pay the

fine we'd have to go to court. The court would send us to jail. The judges in Holland were fed up with this kind of behaviour. I didn't know what to do. Then I remembered the forty guilders.

—John's got money, I said but they didn't understand. I pointed and mumbled about my pal, my friend, he's got money. I made a money gesture with my thumb and fingers. They got it and laughed. I didn't know why they were laughing.

—Your friend, name of John? He has money?

—Aye. Yes, I said.

—You are sure your friend, name of John? He has money?

—Aye! I said.

They laughed again and left talking in Dutch. I don't know any Dutch but I could tell they were talking about me. I heard them going into a room nearby. I looked in the mirror to see if I looked daft. It was hard to tell. I suppose to them I did. I thought I could hear voices again but I wasn't sure.

They came back in angry. John had no money.

—Did ye search him?

They did search him and by the looks of them John didn't take it too well. You could see they'd been in a bit of a struggle.

—You go to court. Will go to prison.

—No wait a minute, I said. —Did ye look in his sock?

—Pardon me?

—It's down his sock the money. Forty guilders.

They didn't understand so I showed them. Took my shoe off and pulled out my sock like a pelican's pouch.

—Down his sock! I said.

They got it now and left laughing again. About ten minutes later they appeared with John and our cases. No sandwiches and no giant Grouse. John never spoke. But he was always like that with the cops. Tight-lipped. Pressured with years of cop-rage. They took us into this room with hundreds of telly screens and told us in funny English no matter where we went in Utrecht station they'd spot us. Then they took us down a long and winding concrete corridor and booted us into the street.

I realised we were actually in a bus station. It was dark and empty except for one bus with its interior lights on. The driver was eating a sandwich. It said Rotterdam on the front.

—I'm starving John, I said, but he never answered. He just walked to the bus and got on. The driver looked at him and turned away. Went back to eating his piece and reading his paper. I got on and he didn't even look at me. I sat on the back seat with John. It was nearly ten o clock. The driver started the bus and drove all the way to Rotterdam. Not another person got on. It was like being in some weird science fiction movie. After half an hour of not saying nothing John stared at me.

—What is it?

—Down his sock?

—What?

—Did ye search down his sock officer?

—What ye on about?

—That was a two way mirror and an intercom. Did ye not hear me shouting when ye were staring into it?

I went into meltdown. It was ages before I could answer. Just me and John and the driver cocooned in that bus and the strange lights of another land spreading away everywhere I looked.

—I was trying to get us out John, I eventually said.

—Fuckin grassing bastard!

—They were going to stick us in the jail.

But John hates grasses. He'd done jail for grasses. He didn't speak all the way to Rotterdam. The driver never said a thing as we got off. He drove away. It was freezing now. Minus fifteen it said on the station wall. And by now the drink had wore off. It was no use. Our dreams of Germany and two big Mercs were dead. I knew if we could get to Europort we could get a lift to Hull from a lorry driver. They're allowed one passenger each and in return you allow them to use your duty free quota.

I asked this guy how to get to Europort. He rhymed off buses and trains. But when I said we were going to walk it, he looked at me as if I was daft. I asked another couple of people and the same thing happened. Eventually I found out Europort was thirty miles away. There was nothing for it and even though John wasn't talking to me I told him we had to walk it.

After a mile I was feeling the weight of my case. But I got a system going. I'd have it in my left hand for a hundred steps and my right for a hundred. John had his on his shoulder, on his head, in different hands but he couldn't get a rhythm. I said about my system but he sneered at me. It was a lot of hate for forty guilders.

We walked all the way there with three incidents. One was when I got the fear in this tunnel that ran under a river estuary. It was tiled in white on the walls, floor and roof and when we reached the middle it disappeared into a point at both ends. It was eternity. The fear rushed over me and I fell on the ground crying. But John kept walking. In the distance his head disappeared in his breath. A headless corpse. And now the voices were telling me to get out of there. I got my case and hurried up after John.

Two hours after that we were walking along this motorway. We had three pairs of socks over our hands now. The only thing keeping us warm was the walking. Then, glory, a cop car drew up. When the cop was talking to John I flung my case in the back seat. I took John's and flung that in too. I got in beside my case but the cop pulled me back out. He flung our cases onto the grass verge. They slid downhill smearing the frost. What the cop was saying, even though it was Dutch, was get off the motorway, you're not allowed to walk on the motorway. He'd arrest us if he seen us again. But he was good enough to give us directions to Europort and tell us we were only twenty kilometres away.

An hour and a half later John let out a roar and flung his case into the river. It sat on the slush a few seconds then gurgled under. An hour and a half after that we came to Europort.

And it was shut.

A sign said it was opening at nine. This was four in the morning. I got my sleeping bag and threw in onto one of them trolley things they use to push luggage about. Even though John wasn't talking to me the two of us got in and cuddled. But it was no use. We were freezing. I got all my clothes out and shared them. Three pairs of trouser and four jumpers each we had on. We wrapped T-shirts round our heads.

We woke up to the thrum of a bus and all these people looking down with amazed faces. We were white. We were a silver sculpture. The sleeping bag was glittering in the morning sun and the T-shirts stiff as cardboard. We were pitiful creaking into that Europort with all them frozen clothes on. We got up next to the heaters and stayed there for an hour. Got talking to a couple of lorry drivers and they liked our story. They laughed so much they called more lorry drivers over. We told it four different times in all. They bought us a breakfast and took us back across to Hull. From there we got a lift in a tanker with this guy who's son had just died in a motorbike crash. He dropped us at Edinburgh and we got a McKechnies Roll van all the way to Glasgow. He dropped us right at the post office where we cashed our Giros to buy the one way tickets.

—That was some round trip, John said.

I smiled and he smiled. He smiled like a pal. But his face was only like that for one frame. If you can measure life in frames. Then he fell back to anger and walked away.

Saturne Monsieur

Amateur fortnight. That's what Connie called Christmas and New Year. She was three years sober and I was three months. Worked in the rehab where I detoxed. She figured a holiday would get us away from the violence and mayhem in Scotland and give us a chance to get to know each other.

—Our bad points, she said and laughed.

—You've not got any bad points, I said.

It was Marmaris and it looked beautiful. There was a big marina with yachts and boats that cost millions. And a bazaar. What I didn't like was all the hasslers trying to drag us into restaurants.

—Breakfast! Full English Breakfast. Come, come eat here so pretty miss.

It was getting me all riled up them tugging and hauling us. I didn't want to make a bad impression on Connie so I smiled and said no thanks.

There was one hassler I didn't like the look of. He had a ragged scar on his face. I noticed the way he held onto her bare arm. When I stepped out in front of him he gave me a predatory look. I threw him a look back and pulled Connie away. I was glad I hadn't let my jealousy show. Connie's ex-husband hospitalised her once in a fit of jealous rage. She's still got the marks. Once we'd ran the gauntlet the beach was great. Waves were falling on the sand and us on our lilos reading books about sobriety. What she didn't know about sobriety you could write on the back of a stamp. And Connie was gorgeous. A wee red bikini and she already had a tan from the sunbed in her spare room. Long dark hair and dark eyes. She could've been Turkish in fact. That's when I realised I'd not seen any Turkish women. Except for big fat ones over sixty. I sat up and looked along the beach. It was all Western women. I wondered where the Turkish women were and asked Connie.

—How – are ye fed up with me already?

—No, I was just noticing that we've not seen any.

That night we walked along the shore to the bazaar. It was dark and a warm wind was streaming in. The stars were out. You could see them sparkling in the water between the hulls. We looked at all the boats in the marina and decided what kind we'd get when we made our millions. The lights were on in some and you could see in. These things were like palaces. In Ariel a millionaire with grey hair and a blue shirt said something to two blonde women and they leaned back laughing.

—How much would one of them change your life? I said.

—It wouldn't change anything.

—What? Sailing about the Med wouldn't change anything? Ye mad?

—For a while aye, they'd change your life, she said. —But not for ever. A boat's not a cure.

She walked away. She had AA answers for everything. If I had a boat like that I'd be fuckin well cured alright. I watched as she strolled in front of me, her heels clicking into the warm night. Ach – what's a disagreement about boats? I caught up and slipped my arm round her waist.

—Who needs boats? I said. —We don't need boats. Boats don't get ye sober.

She squeezed my hand. The tension between us fizzled as we walked over this massive concourse between the marina and the bazaar. It was marble. Holidaymakers were gliding across at all angles. Here and there people had set up their wares. Crepes. Chess sets. Spices. Bangles. Little dogs that barked and danced when you walked past. But there was one man who caught my eye. Even from a distance he was something special. He was stood upright beside a telescope and a chair. Standing like a soldier. No not that – like a butler. That's what he was standing like. Like a head butler. He took a silver flask from his pocket and swigged. He was selling something. But there seemed to be no takers.

When we got there he gave a half bow and swept a white-gloved hand at the telescope. I saw how threadbare his suit was.

—Monsieur Saturne? he said. —Saturne Monsieur.

He could see I was puzzled. He held his white-gloved hands in the sky, framing Saturn for me.

—Saturne? he said. —Saturne Monsieur.

And he pointed to a coin in his palm to indicate the price. He ushered me into the rickety wooden seat and started fiddling with the telescope. He lined it up.

—Saturne Monsieur, he said and swept his arm like he was opening the curtain at the Moulin Rouge. But a cloud came in and covered the sky. I tried to pay but he refused.

—Non. Non. He said and in French told me to come back when the sky was clear. He stood guard by his telescope looking up waiting for the cloud to pass over. When we reached the bazaar I turned and he was still in the same position under the weak spotlight of a street lamp.

The bazaar was marvellous labyrinth of arched tunnels going everywhere. A maze where you could get lost. And the racket of people. And music. And colour. And smell. There was everything you can imagine and a few things you couldn't. Three times we ended up back at the start and only realised it after a minute or two. I didn't mind being pulled and hauled by hasslers in here. That's what bazaars were all about. That's what you expected. Wanted even, for an authentic holiday. It was as if we'd walked into another city. And back in time. Except for the CDs, DVDs, fake iPods, Nike sweatshirts and digital radios that is. We asked the price of a rug and when it was translated into twenty-four thousand pounds we panicked. The bald Turk mistook the look on my face for haggling and dropped to twenty-two. We must've looked like boat owners. We waved no and walked away laughing, feeling like we'd pulled something off.

Connie was trying to buy leather face masks for the punters back at the AA meeting. The guy started talking in what I thought was Turkish. But he came closer and I realised it was English. He was nodding at Connie.

—You sell?

—What?

—You sell wife?

—We're not married.

—You sell beautiful wife – how much?

Me and Connie thought it was funny. He started feeling her shoulders like she was an animal at the market. But he was smiling at me and Connie was taking it in good stead so I pretended to be enjoying it and asked how much.

—Come, come, he said, and went through a green door we hadn't seen. I looked at Connie and she was up for it.

In the back was smaller alleys. Darker and echoing with

the low buzz of the bazaar. And other noises far deep inside. And eerie lights. He wasn't there. I started to see this really was a labyrinth. One wrong step me and Connie'd be lost forever. I started to get the feeling there was something in there.

He appeared with a woman we took to be his wife. Wanted to swap her for Connie. He displayed her by turning her once, then indicated to feel her arms. So I gave the woman's arms a few feels, pushed my bottom lip out and shook my head. I wiggled my fingers at him as much to say, more. Connie couldn't hold her laughing in.

—More? he asked, as if I'd insulted him.

—More, I said.

He went from angry to insulted to gracious, said okay you waiting here, left his wife and disappeared into the gloom. I could hear his footsteps stopping then voices.

—I think he's serious Connie, I said.

—No he's not.

—I'm telling ye, I think he's fuckin serious.

His wife kept staring at the floor. It was tense. Me and Connie stood pulling faces at each other, now and then our feet scratching in the dust. You could see this woman stiffening up as the man came back. He had a girl this time. About the same age as Connie and pretty. He lifted her hair and let it fall. Wanted to give me these two for Connie. The wife could cook and clean and the young one would be good for all the other things. He winked. Connie thought it was great. That it was all craic. But I felt we'd got ourselves in a position. What could I say? No thank you? How insulting is that? He was inspecting Connie again. Touching her thighs, looking at her breasts and making appreciative noises. I knew he expected me to look over the wife and daughter. It was one of the most embarrassing episodes of my life. They just stood there letting me do it. I felt their arms and patted their backs. They smelled of The East. Cinnamon. I didn't dare go near the thighs. Saffron. He had both hands now on Connie's waist and was smiling at me. One of his teeth was gold. I shook my head again. I just wanted out of that place. Back into the safe anonymity of the market.

—Money, he said. —You wanting money too?

He started walking away and I got hold of him.

—No. No money. I have to think.

I tapped my head and he tapped his own back. Maybe that means something different in Turkey, I don't know.

—I have to think about it, I said.

—Ye have to fuckin think about it? Connie said, teasing me.

I told him we'd come back the next night with our decision. He shook my hand, sent the women into the dark labyrinth, and let us go.

We came out into a cacophony of movement and light and let the bazaar carry us off. When we were far enough away we burst out laughing. Connie was hitting me with the bag of leather faces.

—You were going to give me away for that old woman and her daughter.

—I think he was serious, I said.

Next morning we ran the gauntlet. The scarred hassler tried to grab Connie but I pulled her away. On the beach we had a bit of a laugh about how much Connie was worth. We read, discussed all sorts of twelve step books, and slept till the sun was going down. That night we decided to go out for a meal and avoid the bazaar. There might be some law that obliged us to honour a deal once its been instigated. I'd forgot about the Frenchman until he was directly in front of us on the concourse.

—Monsieur Saturne? he said. —Saturne Monsieur.

I was about to say yes when Connie seen the wife seller in the yellow light at the edge of the bazaar. He stared over towards us. Then he waved and started walking over.

—Come on, she said, and we ran laughing through the marina.

We got lost among walkways and boats. Found a secret bay and lay on rocks listening to the sea and looking up to the stars. She was on her back with one leg straight and the other knee up. Her dress had slipped to the top of her thigh and it was turning me on.

—What one is Saturn anyway? she asked.

—Fuck Saturn, I said and jumped on her.

After, we lay back and looked at the stars together. I started to get the feeling that this was the woman I'd spend the rest of my life with.

The next night we were strolling about trying to decide what sort of meal to have. The hassler with the scar grabbed Connie by the arm.

—You eat. You here eat miss. Pretty miss.

His hand on her bare skin. I didn't like it. A hassler from the restaurant across the road got hold of me. Me and Connie were a disconnected tug of war as they swore at each other in Turkish. Connie decided we'd be as well going in the one on her side. We did and left the two hasslers arguing in what sounded like a great language to argue in.

When we were seated I noticed a young Liverpool couple with two kids. His wife was cute and they seemed happy. I hoped I could make Connie happy like that. Then a waiter walked to the Liverpool table. Hovered about smiling. Asking the kids questions so the parents had to respond. You could see they wanted left alone. This waiter he started massaging the woman's shoulders. She kept leaning forward. But he pushed in more. His hands moving onto her neck and back. I could see the decisions on the husband's face. First he was going to attack the Turk. Then he was leaving him alone for the sake of the kids. He looked over and I tilted my palms out as if to say – what can you do mate? The waiter got fed up with monosyllabic answers. He went and spoke to the chef and two other waiters. All the time he was looking at holidaymakers and smirking. I knew he was bad-mouthing everybody in that restaurant. Especially the women. I went on about it to Connie but she wasn't interested. She was too busy looking at the menu. And anyway, in sobriety it's best to mind your own business.

—You've enough of your own battles to fight, she said.

And I suppose she was right. I lifted the menu and tried to understand it.

Then.

Up he came.

Connie shivered when he touched her shoulders. The Liverpool guy looked at me. Connie's flesh indented to the pressure of his fingers. Connie's flesh indented.

Flesh.

Indented.

Chaos broke out. I remember my chair scraping on the tiles. The holidaymakers turned. I reached across the table, grabbed his hands and put two wrist locks on him.

—Get your fuckin hands off my woman! I shouted.

I flung him into the clatter of an empty table. The chef was first to arrive. He had a blade. I lifted my plate and rammed it into his mouth. It disintegrated into shards and

powder. The chef's feet kept coming but the head went
backwards. The knife fell. I stamped and dragged it back.
The waiter ran at me. I sprung up and stuck the head right
on him. Glasgow kiss. The thud echoed round the place. He
curled up whimpering, holding his face.

I heard a siren and thought it might be for me. We left.
We didn't realise another fight had happened outside. We
hid in the crowd. The cops arrived, and an ambulance. The
scar-faced hassler was being dragged fighting to the cop car.
A woman about sixty was on a stretcher; blood running from
her head. Her husband shouting at Scarface. He was going to
kill him. What had happened was the two hasslers continued
arguing when we went into the restaurant. The argument
had built to a scuffle, then Scarface lifted a rock and flung it.
It missed the other hassler and hit an English woman square
on the head. She collapsed. I tried to imagine it. Sitting with
a spoon halfway to your mouth. Talking to your husband.
Relaxed on holiday and bam! A rock sends you onto the
floor. It must be what it's like when a terrorist bomb goes off.
When you're least expecting it. Boom! When you're relaxed.

I came out of my dwam and noticed Connie walking away
towards the bazaar. I caught up.

—Don't go up there, remember the wee guy that wants to
buy you, I said.

But there was no answer. I walked beside her. She had
her arms folded and her head down so her chin was almost
touching her chest. Everybody could see she'd fell out with
me.

—Monsieur Saturne? he said. —Saturne Monsieur.

He guided me to the seat and lined up the telescope. The
sky was clear and this time there it was. Saturn. The rings
clearly visible. It was beautiful. Floating up there in space. It

made me feel peaceful.

—Waw! I said, and looked some more. I leaned out from the telescope.

—D'you want a look?

Connie never answered. She kept on staring at the boats. But this time there was something about these boats that made me feel uneasy. The night breeze was blowing the bottom of her dress.

The Gift

One day in February it was bitter cold. The sky didn't know to drop snow or ice or cold, cold rain so it spewed all three at once. The world outside the chapel house looked cruel and tormented.

It came to my maw as she watched flakes of ice swirling down, how easy it would be to die on the streets. It was as much to do with losing hope as hypothermia. That's why she felt an extra pang of compassion when this pour soul came trudging up the driveway. She knew the crunching was the gravel under his feet but couldn't help feeling it was his bones. The broken remnants of a young man crashing into each other.

—Visitor Father.

—Bring him in Alice.

She opened the door before The Visitor had the chance to knock. Even that was a little blessing. He got to keep his fists in his sleeves. Not to sting his raw knuckles on the bitter wood.

—Come in son ye look freezing, said my maw.

—I'm no bad.

The ice was braiding the fringes of his jacket.

—Want to hang your coat up?

—I'll keep it on.

She brought him to the kitchen where a big old fashioned radiator churned hot air round. If you looked along it longways my maw thought, it looked like the inside of a cathedral. By the time he got to his seat she'd got quite a bit out of The Visitor. His name was Spider.

—This is Spider, Father. He's from here originally.

Father just nodded. It was a kind of joke between Father and my maw. No matter where people have gone in their lives, no matter how far down, there always comes a time when they're driven back home. Searching for something. Father used to say God but my maw thought it was their mother. My maw agreed to disagree on that one. Anyway a search for your mother and a search for God amounted to the same thing.

Spider had his hands shoved into the gaps in the radiator. The ice on the fringes of his jacket was dripping onto the floor. She'd get that later. She gave him an ashtray and a cigarette.

—Just blow the smoke out the window son.

Within a few puffs he was smiling and, she knew, ready to talk. Father wasn't much of a conversationalist. But my maw could talk for Scotland. She waited till Spider had finished his fag.

—D'you want another wee fag son?

—I wouldn't mind missus. That was my first smoke for days.

—Here take the packet.

—No just two would do me hen.

—No here take the packet, I've got another one in my bag.

She couldn't help it. When she said bag Spider looked at it. But her fear diffused because The Visitor she'd thought well into his thirties had the blue eyes of a teenager. And tears welling up.

Spider wasn't planning to steal the bag. He was somewhere else. In the distance. In the past. To bring him back she put the packet of fags in his hand, curled his fingers round them and gave him a lighter.

—You take that son – I got five out the ninety-nine pence shop.

Father was staying vigilant. You had to be on constant alert when a Visitor was in.

—It's cold this weather son, said my maw.

—Aye. Freezing out there. Doesn't look as if it's goanny change an all.

—Where're ye staying the now?

He'd been staying in an old hut up the railway. He'd stapled carrier bags to the roof and made it waterproof. Lighting wee fires on top of a slab.

As Spider told my maw about his past few days Father was to-ing and fro-ing between the house and the chapel. Setting up for a wake. My maw made two rolls on sausage and put them down with a bottle of tomato sauce. He liked tomato sauce so much it came out the sides when he bit into the roll. His eyes narrowed when he closed his jaws so that he looked like a desperate animal.

Turns out he'd been staying in hostels a few years. But they're full of killers and people who need psychiatric help. The longer Spider stayed in one place the more paranoid he got. One day, after a man was found stabbed to death in Spider's room, he got up, rolled his belongings in a sheet and left. Feels safer in disused huts or derelict buildings. But, he says, with the housing boom it's getting harder to find derelicts so sometimes he sleep in abandoned cars or phone boxes.

—Does your mammy live in Cambuslang still Spider?

Having nine wanes herself, she knew his tears were real. She filled his mug with tea and in the silence it sounded like a waterfall.

—She's dead. My mammy's dead.

—Aw that's terrible for ye son. Was it long ago?

He shook out a yes. And held up six fingers.

—Don't talk about it if ye don't want to Spider.

—Call me James. I don't really like Spider.

—Have ye got a father, James?

He nods. He does.

—D'you know where he is?

—He hates me.

—He doesn't hate ye James. That's just you thinking that. He's probably worried sick. When did ye last see him?

He holds up the same six fingers.

—Is he still in this town? Ye can phone him from here.

—He hates me.

—How can a father hate his son?

James looked up. The blue of his eyes.

—I killed my mammy.

My maw's heart took a wee leap. Suddenly the priest and the chapel were a hundred miles away. The sleet smashed on the window.

—W... what did ye do that for son?

—It was six years ago to this very day.

He'd started on smack when he was fourteen. By the time he was sixteen he was a right junkie. His mammy and da tried everything. Locking him in, letting him out, giving him money, keeping him skint, but no matter what they done he got worse. It became too much for them long before his da flung him out. His mammy got home from work one night and felt the coldness in the house. She didn't need to ask. She tried to handle it. But by midnight she had to go out. Searching. Her man tried to hold her back but she struggled out into the snow.

She was amazed at the amount of people moving about. Had any of them seen her James? Some had but they were so drunk or gone with drugs she couldn't follow their directions. Then she remembered one time he'd ran away when he was eleven. His da had slapped him about a bit and he'd took some tins and some candles and off he'd went. She'd found him in an old hut beside the railway.

At that time the fence along the railway was old sleepers. There was one missing. When she seen the small footprints she snuck through and spent five minutes watching him framed in the window. He had a blanket draped over his shoulders and yellow candlelight on his face. He was a painting. When she seen him trying to heat a tin of beans over the candle she had to laugh even though she was crying. Every now and then scooping some out. She opened the door and said she'd come to take him home. His mouth was covered in beans. That was a story James and his mammy shared.

So this night, six years ago, James' mammy made her way to the same fence. There were sleepers missing everywhere. She went from one to the other looking for footprints. But there was footprints everywhere. Some were fresh; others were filled with snow. Others dusting. She came to the same old railway hut. The only thing holding it up was the wind.

James heard feet crunching and tumbled out and ran helter skelter across the railway.

—James. Come back. James – it's me. It's mammy!

But James kept running. Tripping over the lines and getting up. Heard a train and went faster. Could be coming on any line from any direction. Flung himself onto banked up snow. Turned in time to see sparks spraying from the wheels of the braking train. The snow vibrated and there was his mammy framed for death. Looking at James not afraid. As time crushes; emotions expand. James saw his mammy's despair that she couldn't save him. Then she was dead.

Father came in and my maw and him shared a look. She put her arm round James.

—Are ye all right Spider? Is there anything I can get ye? Asked Father.

But Spider wasn't all right. And James wasn't all right. They were both sobbing. Spider who toughed it out on the street. And James who carried an image of his mammy that was crucifying him.

—His name's James, Father. He doesn't like Spider.

James was leaning on my maw's breast. He cried like he'd not cried for years. Father had taken to making the tea and another two rolls on sausage just in case. After a few minutes James came round and thanked my maw over and over. For her understanding. Kept telling her she was a great woman. Reminded him of his own mammy.

—You look just like her in fact, he said, —You're a great woman. What's your name?

—Alice.

—Well Alice – I want to give ye something. I want to give ye a gift. Is it all right if I give ye a gift?

—Aye. That's all right isn't it Father, if James gives me a wee gift?

—Sure, says Father.

James pulled out the biggest steak knife you ever saw.

The blade was eleven inches. My maw didn't have time to jump back but brought her arms up to her chest to fend off incoming blows. But James held that knife with the handle cradled in his right hand and the blade resting in his left. Offered it towards her.

—Here, he said, —I'd like ye to have this.

My maw took it. All the time talking in a friendly voice.

—Oh look Father, James is giving me a lovely knife. Is that not a beautiful knife, Father?

—It is.

—Is it not the loveliest knife ye ever seen, Father?

—It's a great knife, Alice.

—Here, she said, giving the knife to father, —Put it in the DISHWASHER and turn it on.

Father did just that. James stood with a smile on his face. She wrapped up the two rolls on sausage and walked him to the door.

—Just you come back up here any time ye need fed James.

—I will Alice.

James stepped into the snow. My maw looked at the footprints he left and thought of his mammy. The dishwasher was churning in the background. He was halfway down the path when my maw, she shouted.

—James!

He turned.

—Thanks for the knife son.

He waved a no problem and walked on into the gathering snow. She never seen him again.

Tsunami

It was Boxing Day morning and the kids were glued to the telly. A newsflash came on about a tidal wave. Shit! Molly was in Thailand. I'd met her days before when she was here hillwalking. First girl I'd liked since my wife walked out. We spent the weekend together. Should have seen my Out-Laws' faces when I strutted into the Central with Molly on my arm. A model she was like. A pure babe. I could see them asking people who she was but nobody knew. I winked as we left the pub.

Me and Molly went back to my house and shagged all night. I convinced her to stay for the whole holiday and we went to tell her pals. I waited in the hotel bar but when she came down her mood had changed. It was a surprise they'd arranged for her birthday. A backpacking holiday in Thailand. They always got her a good present cos she'd no family except her mother. They wanted to visit The Beach. Pai Pai Island. She said she'd phone before she left. She'd be straight back to Galloway after the holiday. When she didn't phone I assumed she'd got on the plane before she remembered.

The Tsunami didn't seem that serious at first but as the death toll rose I was clicking onto Sky News every ten minutes. There was an uproar cos the kids wanted to see Top of The Pops 2004.

I don't think they noticed anything wrong, even when I took them home early. My ex was still staying with her maw and da at the end of a cul-de-sac you drive downhill into. The snow was a foot thick. The kids battered each other and me and the car with snowballs. I could see somebody at the window. Just a shadow of bitterness. A few neighbours disappeared before I could wave Merry Christmas.

The kids eventually got fed up with snow. Smiling, red-faced and with steam rising off them the two lassies kissed me a Merry Christmas. My son shook my hand. He was trying hard to be a man. The tears he was holding back told me that. He waved before they closed the door. I know I should've been thinking about my kids but all I could think about was Molly. I got in and switched on the radio. Praying she was safe. I had to get home in case she called. But the hill was steep and the wheels just spun making this high pitched growling noise. I let her roll back and attacked that hill. The snow let me ride up then pushed me back like I was nothing. I could feel my Out-Laws watching and was getting all het up. Heavy snow was falling and the more I tried the more of a barrier I was making. The death toll was twenty-five thousand.

And rising.

The Out-Laws' door opened and my son ran out. They tried to stop him but the girls barred their way. He got behind the car and pushed but he was only nine and the car was big and that hill was steep. As I revved, he was a ghost coughing in a cloud of exhaust. I wanted over the crest for his sake. But we never made it. I got out and told him we'd have to dig. Sent him for a shovel and dug the snow with my boot as I waited.

And waited.

He eventually came trudging through the snow. His head was down and he had no shovel. He just shook his head cos he was crying. He didn't need to tell me what happened. I mean a shovel for fucksakes! There was thousands dying the other end of the world. Rolling about in a whiteout of wave. Paradise had disintegrated. And I thought of my marriage. I could remember the paradise but where the tidal wave came from I don't know.

—Da, d'you want me to push again? he said.

—No son. Away you back in and heat yourself up. I'll phone ye the morra.

There was seven houses in that cul-de-sac. At Packie Donnelly's I got no answer even though the light was on. Brolly and Gallagher didn't have a shovel but their paths were clear and their tone was cold. The Retties and the Malarkeys waved me away halfway up their path.

I never even bothered with Curry's. I got in and rolled her back, revved as high as I could and went for it. Throwing a comet tail of snow out and creeping up. But I came to a wheel-whining stop. And if you could've heard me I was screaming Molly's name and crying. All sorts of tears were coming out. Tears of anger at the neighbours who used to be my pals. Tears of dread for Molly. And tears of hate for the Out-Laws. And tears of pure frustration for the snow.

Jean Curry came up with a drink in her hand and rapped her wrinkled knuckles on the windscreen.

—Jean, ye don't have a shovel in there?

—Would you please stop making that racket!

—I need a shovel.

—You've a cheek asking for a shovel ya wife beater.

—What? I said, though I heard it loud and clear.

—Ya worthless bastard. Beating your wife up.

—What ye on about?

—Everybody knows what you done to her.

—I never touched her in my life. Where's all this shite coming from?

—If ye don't desist from this racket I'm calling the police.

—Molly's in Thailand. Molly's in fuckin Thailand.

But she kept staring at me. What the fuck was I telling her that for? She never knew who Molly was. She gave me a funny look, kicked up a cloud of snow, and clicked back along her cleared path. There I was stranded in a white island and hate coming in all around me. The radio said the death toll was now twenty-thousand. I could've lay in the snow and let life run out. That's how I felt. But then there he was, Patrick, running round from the side of the house and dragging the biggest fuck-off shovel you ever saw.

—Da, da here's a shovel here. Here's a shovel!

He dug the corner into the snow at the front wheel. But it was so heavy the shaft was turning in his hands. I got out and took it off him. Started digging.

—Thanks son, you're a lifesaver, I said.

I gave him the job of sitting in the car with the heater on making sure it didn't roll back. Told him to keep his hand on the handbrake and dug two tracks up over the peak of the hill.

The last I saw was Patrick waving and his head sinking under the crest of the snowy hill. I hoped he wouldn't be lost in the wave of bitterness. I hoped he'd stay afloat.

I spent two days watching the email messages pass the bottom of the telly. But there was no Molly from Birmingham. No Molly at all that I can remember. After a few days I got to thinking she must've died. It was a weird feeling. I didn't even know her second name. I thought about contacting her but there was nobody I knew would know her. I called and called her mobile but it was always access denied. I thought of that dead mobile in the white sand at the bottom of the ocean. Days turned weeks into months and I wondered if they ever found her body. She had a mother in London and a father who got five years for nearly killing the mother. No other family that she knew of. So mine was weird grief. Part of me was aching and another part telling me I'd no right. I'd only spent two days with her.

Two days.

Turned out to be a bad year. There are times I wished I'd been in the Tsunami with Molly. My ex taking me for every penny and turning the kids against me.

By the next Christmas I was on pills. My house was being re-possessed. I went on a bender and ended up in Town the Friday before Christmas. It was all a blur. The Out-Laws drew me a disgusted look as I staggered out of the Central. But they were glowing inside. Next thing I remember is the bar in the Waterside. I forced a smile cos it was Christmas and I didn't want to bring anybody down. This pretty thing was chatting me up but I couldn't be bothered. Eventually she moved off. In the flashing lights I thought I seen Molly. But how the fuck could it be? It was only when two of her pals came back from the toilets I seen it was her. It really was her.

—MOLLY! I screamed and ran over. But she turned her back. I went round her and widened my eyes.

—I thought ye were dead?

—Leave me alone, she said.

—What? I thought ye were dead.

—Dead? Why would I be dead?

Her pals were laughing. I wasn't as articulate as I could be because of the drink. I blurted it out. Two words.

—Thailand. Tsunami!

She laughed and so did her pals.

—You didn't believe all that crap did you?

—But you said ye were going – a present – I thought ye were dead. Your phone.

—This phone, she said and held it up. —Access denied, she said, —You wanker! she said.

I suppose my face was a big why.

—I don't like guys who beat up on their wives.

—What?

—They told my pals all about it. You hospitalised her. They should lock men like you up.

—I never touched a woman in my life.

—They told me.

—Who?

—Your wife's family.

—But ye went to Thailand?!

—Leave me alone, she said and walked away. Into the happy Christmas crowd. A wave of nausea came out of that crowd and engulfed me. I was sick splat like that all over that floor.

Voice Mail

Beep. You have three new messages. First message. Monday ninth February at eleven fourteen a.m.

Hello this is Brian here Tony. It's Brian here. Eh – I'm just phoning, just phoning to let ye know. Just phoning to let ye know that's me got it sussed. I've got it sussed see with the drink and all that. The drink Tony. The demon drink. I've stopped. I'm off the drink now. I'm finished with it. That's me. I've got it sussed. Life's great now so it is. Just great Tony. Got my life in order now. Got it all in order. Everything's fine. Just fine. Alright I might have a wee drink when ye publish my stories. When my wee book of stories gets published. When are they getting published by the way? *Buzz*

Beep. Second message. Monday ninth February at three thirty-one p.m.

Well I'm not right off the drink like you. Teetotal and all that. I take a wee drink now and then just. I put soda water in my wine. But I've got it sussed. Life. It's great. Ye can't beat it so ye can't. Life. Life's great. Magic. Things've never been better. I feel great!!! Frosties Cornflakes Porridge Oats and Rice Crispies. Ye can't kid the man that kidded them all cos if ye try to kid the man that kidded them all the man that kidded them all'll kid you – eh? Eh? Like that one? *Buzz*

Beep. Third message. Monday ninth February at ten thirty-six p.m.

Tony it's Brian here. That's me in hospital now. They took me in. Too high they said. For my own good. I'm on Largactil. *Buzz*

Beep. You have one new message. First message. Wednesday eleventh February at nine forty-nine p.m.

Tony it's Brian here. I'm just phoning to tell ye I'm... I'm actually married to Posh Spice. I made love to her on an Apache helicopter last night flying over the Houses of Parliament. The Houses of Parliament. And all the wee people below were looking up. They thought we were terrorists at first but I stuck Posh Spice's arse out the window and they knew what the bold Brian was up to then mate. On ye go Brian they were saying. Get stuck right in there. *Buzz*

Beep. You have one new message. First message. Thursday twelfth February at ten o six a.m.

Just phoning ye to tell ye. It's Brian here. Just phoning to say ye can come up and see me sometime anyway. Visiting is all day. The Godfather now lives at the bottom of the sea and he's called the Codfather. The Codfather. I'm going to make that one of my stories. *Buzz*

Beep. You have two new messages. First Message. Saturday fourteenth February at ten fifty-six a.m.

Hello this is Brian Tony. It's just to say I'm out on home visit. I'm getting my parole. Four and a half hours a day. Seen big Danny at Quiz Night the other night. Trivial Pursuit. Up the canteen. Up Hartwood Hill. He came in third and Ward Twenty-Eight came in... His ward came in third and ours came in second and we got boxes of chocolates and that. Guess what the question was? What do Captain Kirk and Toilet paper have in common? They both get rid of Cling Ons. That's a Trivial Pursuit question Tony I never made that up. It's real.

What was I going to say? Eh? Just to let ye know – to see what's happening with the publication of my stories and that. I'll let ye go. Cheerio! *Buzz*

Beep. Second message. Saturday fourteenth February at eleven twenty-seven p.m.

HELLO!!! This is Brian Tony. Pissed out my head. I'm out on a home visit. My wee brother's got a computer. A new computer that can work as a word processor and put things on disc. It needs a printer for it. And eh... so that was good. I was wondering if ye could phone me back. 01236 seven bananas and an apple. Cheerio! *Buzz*

Beep. You have two new messages. First message. Sunday fifteenth February at four fifteen a.m.

They've took me back in Tony. For my own good they said.
♪ ...the road to nowhere. It's a party Tony.
Get yourself round here with my wee book of stories or I'm coming to get ye. Ha ha.

Danny here's Tony's answering phone... A wee duet Tony.
♪ Burning down the house...
Tony... is that you? It's Danny here.
Buzz

Beep. Second message. Sunday fifteenth February at five o-nine a.m.

He's not there Danny. Listen. What's that noise.
Spaceman! Spaceman!!
Put me down nurse I'm talking to my publisher. *Buzz*

Beep. You have one new message. First message. Wednesday eighteenth February at ten thirty-one a.m.

Hello this is Brian Tony. Just a wee message to say I'm starting writing another book. For a follow up to the one you're publishing. An SAS book and it's called *Go Berserk With Bertie Burke*. Wonder if ye can come up to see me to find out about *Night Of The Wheely Bins*? When it's coming out. My book. If ye can come up and see me. Some night. Maybe Wednesday night eh? No wait a minute – it is Wednesday. Come up tonight then. Ye can bring up the cover. The picture cover. Okay that's all I wanted to say. Just wanted to see the picture cover. Show a few of the patients it. Cheerio. *Buzz*

Beep. You have one new message. First message. Thursday nineteenth February at eleven twenty-one a.m.

Tony it's Brian hee hee hee. *Buzz*

Beep. You have two new messages. First message. Friday twentieth February at two twenty-six p.m.

Alright there Tony? This is Brian. I'm hounding ye again. That's right. I'm hounding ye. Hunting ye down. I'm writing another book called *Go Berserk With Bertie Burke*. It's about the SAS. It's a cracking story. Every bit is intriguing. I'm going to try and do about thirty pages of it. I'm going to try and do about two pages a day. So I'm working on a longer novel. Know something – I'm sick of talking to this answering phone of yours. I'd like a wee chat with ye. I'm out on home visit just now. I'm at mum and dad's house waiting for the game to come on and eh... that's all I've got to say. *Buzz*

Beep. Second message. Friday twentieth February at eight fifty-four p.m.

Watching *Alias Smith and Jones* just now on Sky. All I want to say is as long as my book comes out – *Night Of The Wheely Bins* – I'll be happy. Over the egg and spoon – that's the moon. I want to see the picture cover. The picture cover. I want a copy of it in my house. Then ye can take as long as ye want with the book. The picture cover, that's all I want. Picture cover. Picture cover. And eh. All the money. All the money from the sale of the book can be put into mental health. I don't want much. I'd like to invest it in mental health. Invest it Tony OK. 01236 seven bananas and an apple. Phone us. That's my number. You know my number anyway ya freak. I've got an overnight pass. Cheerio! *Buzz*

Beep. You have one new message. First message. Saturday twenty-first of February at seven forty-three a.m.

Hello this is Brian, Tony. I know you're busy, eh... weighing page three girls. But eh, I'll just let ye go and maybe get ye sometime. It's just that I'm writing a brilliant book called *Go Berserk With Bertie Burke*. About the SAS. I'll let ye go then. Ye should read this stuff. It's high, top material. I'll see if I've got time to finish it in hospital, try and do about forty or fifty pages. Alright Tony? It's just to ask – if I'm writing it, would you be able to transfer it onto disc? Ye don't live that far away. My wee brother's got this computer and I'm writing it onto that on my home visits. I'm talking about in six months time. Cheerio. *Buzz*

Beep. You have one new message. First message. Tuesday twenty-fourth of February at nine nineteen a.m.

Hello Tony this is Brian. Just wondering if ye could come up and see me sometime? I've wrote a good few pages of this *Go Berserk With Bertie Burke*. But they all think I'm mad in here. It's a good book. Brilliant so it is. Very intriguing. Ye should read it. You'll like it. I'll let ye go. *Buzz*

Beep. You have one new message. First message. Friday twenty-seventh of February at ten thirty-six p.m.

Hello this is me Tony, Brian. Just to say I had a long night out last night. I was out. I had escaped. Helicopters an that were looking for me. Ended up turning myself into Monklands Hospital. I was on my way to your house. Just to have a wee talk like. Nothing – sinister. And eh... it was me that named Don Quixote. Is he good, is he bad, or just crazy

– I added the crazy bit to the end of that song and nicknamed him Don Quixote. I'm just wondering if ye can come up. Bring my book. Bring *Night Of The Wheely Bins* if ye can. That's all I've got to say. Tell your wife I was asking for her. Is she still a babe? That sweet woman. I'd like to see her playing *Always Look on the Bright Side of Life* on her guitar. That'd be good if she could come up and maybe give us a wee show? Stand outside the window and busk. On the grass outside the ward. Play the guitar and maybe do magic tricks like we done in Buchanan Street that time. Cheerio Tony. *Buzz*

Beep. You have one new message. First message. Saturday twenty-eighth of February at ten twenty-five p.m.

Hello this is Brian here Tony. Thanks for the letter. There's no address on it. Have ye moved? Send me your new address so me and some of the patients can visit. Only kidding. I'll come myself. I'm feeling quite merry and it's cheered me up that my book's finally going to come out soon in April. That's great so it is. Great. I hope ye get it finished in time. I want to show it to all these loonies in here. An eh... just wishing ye all the luck. And I was going to say – I'd like to invest any money I make off the book directly back into mental health. That would be my reward. That's right! That's all I want. That's all I wish to say. Cheerio! *Buzz*

Beep. You have one new message. First message. Monday the second March at five twenty-two p.m.

Hello this is Brian Tony. Just wondering when you're coming up to see me. Eh... I know it's been snowing lately so ye couldn't come up but eh... I was wondering if ye could come up and see me and bring up my picture cover and a few of my stories. If ye can. Picture cover. For the other patients. They don't believe me. That's all. Cheerio! *Buzz*

Beep. You have one new message. First message. Thursday

the fifth March at nine fifty-nine p.m.

Hello Tony, this is Brian. Just wondering when you're coming up to see me. To bring the picture cover of my book up. That's all I'm asking for. *Buzz*

Beep. You have one new message. First message. Saturday the seventh March at nine forty-five a.m.

I'd like for ye to come up when you're seeing Big Danny and that. Eh... I'm on close obs the now because I went and kicked the television. That's close observation. Suicide watch. I was angry at the situation with the book. *Magic Roundabout* Tony. Take that Zebedee!!! I says and tunnelled it with my leg. But I'm a lot better. I'm a lot better now. They're taking the stitches out tomorrow. And the new medicine's working. I'm on chlorine or something. I'll let ye go then Tony. *Buzz*

Beep. You have one new message. First message. Wednesday the eleventh March at two sixteen p.m.

Hello Tony this is Brian. Just to keep making sure that I'm still on the spot with the book and eh... come up and bring the picture cover. I know it's terrible weather. But when you're up to see Big Danny ye can pop in and bring my book. The cover. If it's out in March. If ye get it for March the twenty third. I know the launch is April the twenty third but it's just the picture cover I want to see. That's all. I should be out soon. I'll try and get parole. By the way I just realised how could you have moved? It's still the same number for the answering phone. Ye still live at the same address. *Buzz*

Beep. You have one new message. First message. Thursday the twelfth March at eleven thirty-six p.m.

Hello Tony this is Brian. I'm getting out for the weekend. I'm coming up to see ye. I'll just wait in your garden till ye come in if you're not there. I don't want to sit in the house alone with your wife. I'm not supposed to be alone with women. Wonder why? Ha ha. If you want to get in touch with me phone the payphone here. Ask for me Tony, Brian. Some of them just look at the phone here so tell them to put it down and phone again. Say, Put the phone down. Put-the-phone-down. Say it dead slow. Okay. *Buzz*

Beep. You have one new message. First message. Saturday the fourteenth March at twelve thirty-four p.m.

Hello Tony this is Brian phoning. Wow man. I'm really delighted with the book cover. Really delighted. Really made my day. Really brilliant so it is. Brilliant. Absolutely brilliant. I'm looking at it right now. Get in contact with me whenever you're ready – right? So I can thank ye, right? Fabulous. Ye can tell me what's going on. Absolutely brilliant! Aye my mum goes like that when I got home – I've got a wee surprise for ye up the stair – I didn't know what it was! Then I came up and eh... GOD!!! I saw

Night Of The Wheely Bins

by

Brian McNee

That's me the Don now eh!? He he. So I'll let ye go then Tony. Cheerio. I can't get over it I'm just... I'm just... Thanks. That's you in my good books now. *Buzz*

Fountains

Even though it was November the sun was warm on the cobbles.

Five sunny cobbles, ten sunny cobbles, twenty sunny cobbles...

You could almost feel it through the soles of your shoes.

Thirty sunny cobbles, forty sunny cobbles, fifty sunny cobbles...

I had three hours before my next meeting so I was wandering about London counting things to keep my mind off terrorism. I came up this skinny alley and found myself facing a building that looked like an old friend. It took me five or ten seconds to realise it was the Law Courts that were on the news every night. I just didn't recognise them without a man with a microphone and a bunch of people with placards.

As I counted the steps into the court I could hear water. For all I knew it could be a river. But I could hear water.

I could hear water.

I could definitely hear water. Was there a river under my feet? I listened intently. In this water was the voices of children. High pitched and happy like playing on a beach. It – was – coming – from –

Behind me!

Behind me was a close and through it was a sun lit courtyard. People were lounging about drinking Seattle Coffee and eating sandwiches on ornate sandstone benches. If it was Scotland it would be spring. But it was November and it was London.

I went in and found myself a seat. The river turned out to be a hundred fountains coming up in single spouts straight from the ground. In that sandstone courtyard, blocking out the breath of winter, it felt like France. And these fountains were in some sort of grid. The size of half a football pitch. The spouts coming up randomly. I sat mesmerised trying to find me a pattern. And every time I felt a pattern emerging, the sequence, if I can call it that, changed. There was no pre-empting this.

Some people sat around chatting, others clearly had troubles to mull over and some were like me, taken by the water. Its sound, its shimmering silverarity. When they rose up, before they flowered out at the top, these spouts looked like metal rods. Some amazing metal yet undiscovered. Then they'd trumpet out and fall around themselves in a glassy veil, then they'd be gone. There was always twenty-five in the air at any given time. But which twenty-five? I unfocused and tried to take in the whole vista at once.

There must be a pattern. There must be a pattern. There must be a

pattern.

A scream. Everybody turned cos these are nervous times. But it was only two young girls and they were racing through the fountains. Sorry, not through them; over them. They were running the lines. Zig-zagging and changing lanes but always on the grid of spouts. When the first one got blasted she screeched and laughed, blinking and rubbing her eyes.

Standing in the sun varnished with water. Her pal, she was about ten, doubled over laughing and pointing then they were obscured behind new spouts.

They went back to the beginning. Got in sprinting positions.

—Three, two, one, go!

Off they went. Straight for a bit, splitting off at ninety degrees, then another sharp ninety but always moving, never looking back. Halfway they got sloshed simultaneously. They turned with shoulders up and arms hanging down making a sound halfway between crying and laughter. Then they smiled and I swear the sun got brighter. Even though them two girls were shivering, any cold in the air disappeared. When they got back in sprinting position everybody in that courtyard was watching.

—Three, two, one, go!

Off they went turning and twisting with greater grace this time. Halfway one of them got caught but her pal kept going. She took a right. Took a left. Two leaps forwards, and all the time the water spouted just behind her. But the water couldn't catch her. She was one step ahead of chance. In a ballet of total intuition. We were all open-mouthed willing her on.

—Go on Burton, her pal shouted. —Go on!

The water was running off her but she knew Burton was onto something. She yelped and shouted. —Keep going.

We were on the edge of our seats.

That's when I realised what it was. These girls trying to cross over in the ever changing rods of water. And if they get wet?

So be it.

So be it.

If they get wet. So be it. So me, and the pretty young professional on the bench beside me, and everybody in that courtyard was transported to when we ran through fountains screaming. When we were not afraid of drops of water on our suits or our hair sticking to our foreheads. That day, the pang of loss pealed round that square. Somewhere we'd been swept away on the surface of life and the breathtaking obstacles of our youth turned from water, to wood, to stone. We were dead and here was life.

When Burton burst out the other end we all cheered.

—She done it, said this girl next to me. —She bloody well done it. And she stood up and began applauding.

I have to say I was embarrassed at first by that.

—Well done! she shouted. —Well done little girl!

But another woman stood and clapped. Then two men. Then we all stood. When I clapped I meant it. I really did mean it. Burton took the standing ovation with a series of over emphasised bows.

Her pal caught up and hugged her. It was a moment that couldn't be topped that day. Or even that week. Or maybe the whole year. Who knows, I was thinking, maybe it'll stay with me my whole life, them two wee girls and the fountains.

But then

A red-haired woman in her forties steps into the fountains and, walking at first she gets faster, winding her way towards the children who are laughing and wet.

Road Rage

This was long before road rage was actually invented. It was early March in 1987. I was on steroids and had a wee Peugeot 104. It was a wreck. No tax, MOT or insurance. But there was something about me then that was reckless. My life had kinda went down the tubes and there was a lot of anger tornadoing about inside me.

That wasn't helped by the testosterone injections I was giving myself daily. I was a man-meat mountain and was even scared of myself. It's easy to see it all now but then it was just a vague feeling of unease and the pressure of anger from my solar plexus. I suppose I was dangerous. And paranoid. Boy was I paranoid. If you looked at me, you were threatening me.

—The fuck're you looking at?

Usually nothing was the answer. Head down and away with me shouting. It didn't matter if there was one, two or ten. I'd go for them like a rabid dog.

My maw asked if I could run her into the Royal. She wasn't sure how the buses would be running with this Siberian weather we'd been having and her appointment was at nine. She'd recently had an unexpected heart attack and they were trying to get to the bottom of it.

—Fucksakes maw, that's the rush hour. It'll do my head in.

—Don't bother, she said. —I'll just walk up to the Mill Brae
and get a bus.

And she let me know what that meant. It meant getting
up at seven. It meant leaving the house at half past. It meant
trudging through snow and ice up that steep hill. It meant
standing freezing with the throng of workers. It meant a
stop-start stressful journey into Glasgow. If the bus even
made it in this weather that is. If the bus even turned up in
this weather, that is. If the bus didn't leave them stranded for
hours on top of that windy hill, that is.

—Alright! All right for fucksakes, I said.

—Thanks son, she said with her big mammy smile.

—Make us a couple of rolls on sausage, I said.

And as she fried them up she asked if I could drop Wendy
off at uni. Only she called it University, my maw.

—So long as she doesn't burst my head with all that
feminist shite.

—She's not a feminist any more. She gave it up, says my
maw.

I picked them up at quarter to eight next morning. Cup of
tea and two rolls on bacon waiting for me.

—Alright Wendy?

—Alright steroid man, she said and posed a double bicep.

I ignored her. But as I was drinking my tea she said it,

—Smashed anybody's head in lately?

—Fuck up you.

—Violence, violence, violence.

—If people would leave me alone I wouldn't need to be
violent.

—People can't leave you alone, she said. —We live in a,
and she paused before she said it —Society.

—Not according to Thatcher, I said.

—Taking an interest in politics she said. —There must be some brain cells in there.

Knock, knock, knock she went on my head.

—What ye fuckin on about? Taking an interest in politics doesn't make you clever ya lezzy.

—My sexual preference is my business.

—Lezzy!

—Says the guy that gets big Vic to inject him in the arse.

—I do my own injections, I said.

Or spat really cos by now I was right next to her with my skin stretched to across my cheekbones.

—Get your big false-tan face out of my breakfast, she said.

I sat down and tore a chunk out of my roll on bacon.

When we walked down to the car my maw and Wendy were linking arms and holding each other up on the ice. I opened the passenger door and let my maw in the back. Wendy stood behind me.

—I can open doors myself thank you.

—I never opened for you ya fuckin nutter. I opened for my maw.

I left it wide and went to my side. She waited till I sat down before she got in and slammed that door hard.

—Is that door shut? I asked and she sneered.

So just to give her something to moan about I picked up speed into the cul-de-sac and done a sweet handbrake turn with my maw screaming Jesus Christ what's he up to now in the back and Wendy delivering a little sarcastic applause.

Nothing was said till we got to the Mill Brae. There was over a hundred people there. The buses obviously were well out of kilter.

—See, I was right son. I'd've been standing there for hours, missed my appointment.

—And I would have missed my lecture, said Wendy.

—What's it on? Annoying cunts? I said.

—The battle against misogynist society.

—What the fuck's that when it's at home?

—Taking the world back from people like you, she said.

—Ye can fuckin have it!

Although it was snow falling on ice, there was enough snow for the wheels to get a bite. And here and there the salt had burned a couple of hundred yards of good traction, setting you up for the next run of ice. A few times we skewed into the kerb with a yelp from my maw and some remarks about testosterone from Wendy.

—Aye, I said lifting my eyebrows. —That's what I'm injecting myself with. And making like a monster out some science-fiction movie I said to her, —Soon there will be not a lezzy left on the planet!

—Oh Vic! Vic, can you stick this big phallic symbol in my bum please!

—Stop this filthy talk, said my maw and flung in a Jesus Mary and Joseph.

We fell silent. It was only the scrunching of the wheels in the snow. So I gave Wendy a hundred decibels of Springsteen to cope with and we rolled towards the centre of the city.

As we closed in on the Royal the traffic was grinding to a halt. Slow slow slow. But it was only half-eight and my maw was well on time. Then I had to get onto the main drag. They were letting us through one at a time. But when it came my turn this Sierra with four guys cut me off. Didn't let me though. I raised a hand and shouted,

—Thanks a fuckin million ya cunt.

And, as Wendy told me how offended on how many levels she was by the word cunt, the four of them were giving me streamed up abuse that I couldn't hear.

I rolled the window down.

—What was that? I shouted.

Their electric windows sailed down and they called me all sorts of pricks and wankers.

—Just ignore them son, said my maw.

But as Wendy shook her head I was out the car in a fog of testosterone. One of them opened the door and made like he was getting out.

—I'm goanny rip you ya cunt, he said.

But I was heat seeking. And when he seen that thing in my eyes that's been bothering me my whole life he got back in and the windows sailed back up. I pressed my face to the glass.

—Get out the car!

No answer.

—Get out the fuckin car, I said.

No answer. I booted a panel in. They tried to spin away but the cars were nose to tail. I booted another panel. The driver opened his door. —That's my fuckin car! he said.

—Is it?

Bang! Another panel.

—You're fuckin getting it, he said. But as I ran round he got in and gunned the engine. It was snaking and going nowhere. I got my hand on the handle and one foot on the car and tried hauling that door open. The muscles were ripping through my skin. I had tunnel vision for opening that door. It's probably hard to believe but I was crying with rage. Then I noticed the car moving. All the snaking had moved them to where they could get onto the other side of the road. Traffic was piling into Glasgow, but hardly any was coming out. They sped away with me hanging on.

So there's me, one foot on the driver's door, both hands on the handle, his wheels spinning, trying to get some traction on the ice and my right leg skating along. Three guys shouting for the driver to get out of there. When the wheels hit a bit of salted road they shot forwards and I fell off. They gathered speed in a horrible nightmare slowness as I got up, ripped a paling from a metal fence and made towards them. At first I was gaining. Then we were moving at the same speed. Then they began moving away. I spun the paling but it only bounced off the boot as they made their way down Queen Street in the face of oncoming traffic.

—Bastards! I screamed. When I turned it was gridlock Glasgow at the Royal Infirmary. My wee red car askew on the road with the driver's door flung open.

And the passenger door.

And the passenger door.

And there was my maw and Wendy skidding across the ice trying to get away. They couldn't sit no more with the traffic piling all around them watching and something about to happen.

Something

About to happen.

They Scream When You Kill Them

Joe brung the langoustines. He'd asked me the other day
down at the harbour if I wanted some and even though I
never knew what they were I said:

—Aye bring me some round.

—They're great with a chilli sauce, he said.

About a week or so after that I heard the drill of a diesel
engine outside. The door went, the dogs barked and the
cats jumped onto the kitchen units. It was Joe and he was
in a hurry. His driver's door was flung open. Had to go up
to Troon. Deliver the lobsters, pick up his bait. I'd forgot all
about the langoustine conversation and wondered why he
was handing me this bright red bucket. It was half-filled with
water and all these wee orange fellahs. At first I thought
they were baby lobsters because that's what they look like,
langoustines. I took the bucket, said cheers and he shouted
chilli sauce as he was driving up the street.

Connie puzzled when she seen the bucket.

—Joe's brung us these, I said and sat the bucket on the
floor. She bent down looking in. So did I.

—Langoustines? she said.

They were a bright orange that's hard to explain. Maybe
it was the red of the bucket reflecting on them but they
looked like cartoons. There was at least fifty going every way

possible in that confined space. You could see they weren't used to moving about in hardly any water. Some swam frantically crashing into the sides. Others sat on the bottom looking up. Others were still and might've been dead.

—He said they're good with chilli sauce.

—They're alive.

—Some of them.

—Most of them, she said, and swirled the water. The agitation caused the still ones to move their limbs. We watched them in silence with water slipping off her hand back into the bucket. She'd been spending a lot of time in the garden with the other three cats since we buried Floyd and the tan on her face was burnished by the red glow from the bucket.

—I think ye just drop them in boiling water like lobsters.

As soon as I said it I knew it was the wrong thing. Still crouched down she put one hand on her thigh and looked up.

—Ye can't drop them in boiling water – have ye ever heard the noise a lobster makes?

She stood up.

—They scream when you kill them, she said.

—No they don't, I said.

She pointed to our dogs, a collie and a lurcher.

—How would you like it if somebody dropped one of them into a pot of boiling water?

—That's different.

—Is it?

—Okay then, I said. —Let them die. They'll die naturally. Then we'll cook them.

She looked at me and went out into the garden. I heard her walk across the grass and I knew where she was going. I sat for a while in the quiet cool of the kitchen watching the langoustines. I don't know how long it was but they moved less and less until they were all still. When they were all dead I crept closer. But they exploded, their claws and feet rattling on the sides of the bucket. They weren't going to die easy.

I made a pot of tea. The sun was coming in sheets through the half-shut blinds. I knew Connie was staying in the garden out of the way so I took her tea out. She was sitting beneath the cherry trees beside Floyd's grave. Connor, our collie, was watching her every move. She looked up and I could tell even from halfway down the path that she'd been crying again.

—Well?

—Not yet, is all I said, and put the tea on a stone.

When I got back to the kitchen our big lurcher had his head in the bucket like a giraffe. Fishing.

—Bailey!

His hairy head popped out, water pouring off. A langoustine struggled in his front teeth. He was holding it delicately and staring at me.

—Leave it!

No way, was the look on his face. He slunk down and his tail curled under. He let out a growl.

—Leave it Bailey!

I moved to get the langoustine and crunch. It fell on the floor in two halves. The head part was running away on these long spindly legs. For a moment I could see it all from the langoustine's point of view and it was horrific. Bailey warned me away with a snarl, scooped the tail up and ate it. Then, as he grabbed the head, I noticed Connie in the doorway. Bailey pushed past her growling and into the garden to nibble away at his catch.

—Did you give him one of them?

—No.

—Ye gave him one didn't ye?

—I came in and he had his head in the bucket. I couldn't get it off him.

She shook her head.

—He was like that (snarl) going to fuckin bite me. Ye know what he's like – he's a thieving bastard.

Connor hated tension in the house. He came to me then Connie nuzzling and kissing and asking us please be pals. Please be good. Please stop arguing. And he won't stop until you truly are calmed down. So we did. It's the only way to stop him. If you've got a collie you'll know what I mean. Once we were calm he took to wagging his tail fascinated by the things in the bucket. Connie hadn't looked since she came in from the garden.

—Are they dead yet?

I swirled the bucket and they weren't. The water was getting warm. She wasn't for waiting out in the garden while I let a bunch of wee animals die in the house. I suggested to put them in the freezer, see if that would kill them quicker but that's not where she wanted the conversation to go. She stared at me. I knew what she was going to say and was searching for answers before she said it.

—We'll have to put them back.

—He catches them way out at sea. What d'you want me to do – swim out with the fuckin bucket in my teeth?

—The sea's the sea. Put them in on the beach. I'm not letting them die.

And she looked for the first time since she came in. So did I and guilt flooded me. I'd try to tell myself it was okay. I wasn't killing them. They were dying themselves. As if that's what they were choosing to do. But she was spot on. It just felt wrong us letting them die right there on that kitchen floor.

So, we put Bailey and Connor in their room. Threw two trays of ice into the bucket. Covered it with a black bin liner. Connie went out to open the boot and check for people. The signal was three knocks and out I came holding the bucket to my chest. The langoustines were sloshing about. I placed it carefully in the boot and clicked it shut. The sun was blazing.

—Joe better never find out about this, I said.

We drove ultra slow down South Street, so slow that a caravan driver was agitated behind us. I made some kind of joke about the irony of that but she was focused on releasing these wee fellahs. We wound our windows down but the heat was still unbearable. We drove round past the harbour onto the shingle beach that faced England. It was almost impossible to be seen from there. Almost. Just as I opened the boot Tin Tin came out of nowhere with Floss.

—Aye! he said.

I snapped the boot shut.

—Some day Tin Tin, I said, —Hot.

He sensed my agitation and nodded at the boot.

—What's in there – a body?

—No, just wasn't shut right.

Connie started throwing stones into the sea for his dog. Tin Tin watched Floss swimming for ages then walked away talking to himself. Floss followed, shaking rainbows off her fur. But by then four holidaymakers had arrived with a picnic basket. We got back into the car and reversed off the beach.

—Go round the other end, Connie said.

The village is on a horseshoe bay a half a mile or more across. At the other end a long line of yellow sand comes to a point at the trees. We couldn't see anybody.

When we got there it was empty. We opened the boot but I started to get paranoid. The whole village with its painted houses stood across the bay looking at us. It was like trying to get rid of a body. The bucket sat there ominous and none of us could lift it. Connie felt the water.

—It's getting warmer. I don't want them to die!

—Fuck it, I said and lifted the bucket. But she heard something and pushed it back in. We scanned the bay. The noise had come from the trees. It could be cattle or there might be somebody in there watching. Truth was, there was nowhere secluded on that whole bay. No matter where you went someone spotted you. The only secrets were the ones you kept inside your head.

We were beat. The langoustines were dying and the tide was on the ebb. I tried to think of other points where you could get down to the sea with a car but I couldn't. The only ones I could suggest were so far away that they would all be dead before we got there. Then I noticed Connie was crying.

—Ye shouldn't've took them in the first place, she said.

—Oh aye, blame me cos a guy does us a favour.

—Ye should've said no.

—How the fuck could I say no – I didn't even know what they were at the time.

—So ye told him to bring things ye didn't have a clue about?

—No – I didn't tell him anything. He asked me and rather than offend him I said aye.

—What if they were big fuckin things like alligators?

I thought of a bucket of alligator heads snapping at me and burst out laughing. So did she. We gave each other a hug and I suppose from across the bay we looked like a couple making up after an argument. Then I had an idea.

230

—The stream, I said.

—What?

—The stream. Drive along the stream and when we're far enough out of the village dump them in there. They'll make their way back to the sea no problem.

She thought it was a great idea. We rushed off at ten miles an hour. Both our windows were down with the heat. The stream runs for two miles alongside the road into the village. We waved to a few passing villagers who were probably talking about the argument we'd just had at the end of the bay.

When we got far enough out I stopped. A car went past and flashed its lights. I waved. Then it was all clear. Connie got out, opened the boot, grabbed the bucket, disappeared through the trees and down the slope. I heard her mashing about in the mud then a pour and a splash – like somebody being sick. There was nothing for a few moments and I was beginning to think she'd fell in when up she came through the bushes with a big smile. There was mud halfway up her shins with a perfect line at the top. She got in and put the bucket at her feet.

—Lost my shoes. Stuck in the muck.

She was breathing hard with elation and relief. The bad feeling was gone. I leaned across and kissed her. Told her she was a lifesaver.

—Did they swim away? I asked.

—Some of them were dead. I think. They washed away with their arms hanging down like this. But the rest of them turned and faced the sea and swam. Should've seen them. They were like wee orange compasses. And they say animals are daft.

—At least we've saved most of them, I said.

She kissed me and said —Next time just say no.

I nodded and we drove off down that long straight road passing the langoustines. Then a thought came to me. An urge to go to the bridge and see them coming under it. I know it's daft but I wanted to see if there was any change in their expressions when they sensed a trace of salt water in their nostrils – if they've got nostrils. It had been some day for the wee guys. From the lobster creels to a bucket – the big lurcher monster fishing for them, the journey in the boot of the car and the slosh into a freshwater stream. It would be just magic to see their faces when they surged into that ocean and freedom. Connie thought I was mad.

When we got to the bridge, I was about to swing the door open and jump out when a car came round. It was Joe.

—Shit, said Connie and tried to hide the bucket under her legs.

—Awright, he said.

—That was quick – Troon.

—Roads were empty, he said. —Did ye eat the langoustines?

—Aye! We both said at the same time. Joe was a bit taken aback with the ferocity of our answer. The langoustines were probably passing underneath us at that point. Then I let fly.

—Had them with chilli sauce right enough. Aw they were great. A wee bit of lemon an all they were great weren't they Connie? Weren't they great eh?

—Aye. Brilliant.

—Right, Joe said.

I think he could see the bucket. But he never said anything. He just said he'd bring us some more next week.

Hang Jim Davis From A Sour Apple Tree

Jim was in good fettle and started on about the shite on the telly. Then this nun appeared and the way the conversation went you knew they had history.

—How are you, James?

—Never been better, he said.

—That's a change. And what are you going to do today?

—I'm goanny fling a cow over the moon.

I knew, and he knew, and the nun knew exactly who that cow was.

—My, my James, now what d'you want to go and do a ting like that for now?

—Cos it's been annoying the life out of me for weeks sister.

—Has it now?

—Aye – it has now.

—And how are you going to get it back? After you fling it all the way to the moon this poor ting?

—With a lot of persuading, he said. —I'll get that cat with the fiddle to help me.

I started laughing and this nun, who up till now thought I was on her side, her face fell and she said she'd drop in later.

—Make it through the roof, Jim said and she left. Then he turned on me.

—Where have you been?

—Been busy.

—You said you'd visit me once a week and I've not seen ye for months.

—Know why that is Jim?

He didn't.

—Cos I'm a selfish bastard and you're a crabbit bastard.

We laughed. Too long and too loud for a place like that. He got me to move the big photo of his grand-wane so he could see it better then he asked me to move his feet. When I lifted the blanket he had socks on. Scooby Doo socks they were, like the kind you get for Christmas.

—Scooby Doo?

—Grand-wane bought us them.

—Where d'you want them? Left, right, up, down – what?

He directed me so his feet went exactly where he wanted. That seemed to relax us both and we sailed right on into the old stories.

The time I bust all his new drums for no reason I can think of. And neither could he.

The times my da used to tie him and Boon to the leg of the table with their reins to keep them under control.

The time he broke his arm when Daniel pulled him off the top shelf of the cupboard.

The time I was drinking out the tap and my da slapped me on the back of the head and when I turned with two broken front teeth I was Jim.

The time he met the UFO and they said all faired haired ones come to me and a labrador walked on and it flew away. How that terrified me and my fair hair for years.

The time he walked the plank on the building site and fell, and the plank fell edgeways onto his head. And I carried him bleeding into the Monklands Bar and drunk men took charge.

The time we were altar boys and we stole the wine and looked for God in the tabernacle. He was nowhere to be seen.

The time he showed me how to sniff shookie from the cuff of my Columba RC High blazer.

The time we broke into the Rowntree McIntosh factory and filled black bin bags with Walnut Whips and we took to biting the walnuts off and throwing the whips at passing trains.

The time he made it onto the front page of the *Advertiser* as Glue Sniffing Den discovered. He was famous.

The time we contacted the spirits and the wane lifted three feet off the couch and me and big Owensy ran three miles home in the dark.

The time we bought a bottle of Lanny and drank till we were sick.

The time we stole all the flashing lights from the roadworks on the main street and got caught cos Brian McGilliard had them in his room flashing like a house fire.

The time he joined the Merchant Navy and they wouldn't let me in cos I had a record.

The story about him and Rab and the hammer head sharks in Mawadyboo bay.

The time he walked in with that babe of an absolute beautiful bird. She was Miss Barrhead and his chest was out. Our chins were down. And oul Mary said – Barrhead? A buckin bridge and a bus stop!

The time when he was just married and me and him had the Hoover emptied on the floor searching for a lost gram.

The time he just disappeared and nobody heard a peep

– not even oul Mary.

The time he was in London and three guys got him cornered in an alley and he just said – I've a hard life. And they left him alone.

The time he turned up with the funny wee Jesus Army jacket on – praising the Lord outside ASDA and I blanked him.

The time I found God and told no cunt cos of the way they ridiculed him and his Jesus Army.

The time in the monastery when Jim was saying the Devil wrote the Bible and the monk said, Dearie, dearie me, is that the postman, I'll have to go make his tea.

The time we went to Ireland with a poof, a Malaysian girl and two lezzys and him on his guitar as good as Clapton but undiscovered.

The time, in his band, when he used to sing instead of Addicted to Love: you've really got to face it you're a dick!

The time he found out he had the big C and told my maw not to tell anybody.

The time his daughter turned up after eighteen years.

The time he found out he was going to be a granddad.

The time he held his grandwane. Aye – the time he held him.

The time I brought that Hillbilly song into the hospital – Hang Jim Davis From a Sour Apple Tree to the tune of John Brown's Body. And we laughed about just how apposite that was that day in them circumstances and we played it and we sang. With tears in our eyes we sang.

We went through a lot by the time that cow came back down from the moon and I had to go. He asked me to move his feet again before I left.

—Can you feel your feet Jim?

—Aye.

—Ye can actually feel them? Even with the epidural?

—A bit, he says.

—Can you feel this? And I ran my nail up the sole of his sock.

—Hey that's fuckin tickly, he said.

—Is it now?

So I done it again.

—Fuckin stop it, he said but he was laughing so much I started on the other foot.

—What about this one?

—Nurse, nurse, he was shouting but the tears were coming down his face.

I tickled him till the two of us were blue. When I stopped we were laughing like the two wee boys we used to be. When I stopped laughing I still had hold of his feet.

—Right where d'you want them?

—Over that way a bit.

But I held on for too long. His heels were cupped in my hands and we looked at each other. And he couldn't talk either he just nodded with this smile. I put his feet down. Pulled his socks up, his pyjamas down and fixed the blanket.

—See ye Seamus.

—Aye. Sometime.

The last thing I done was wink. I don't know why I done that but he winked back and I walked away. I could feel him watching me all the way up that corridor but I never turned back.

And now. I'm a hundred miles away from where we grew up. And I'm sitting with my mobile phone trying to delete Jim Davis. But somehow I can't believe that I have to.

Some other books published by **LUATH** Press

The Glasgow Dragon
Des Dillon
ISBN 1 84282 056 7
PBK £9.99

Nothing is as simple as good and evil.

When Christie Devlin goes into business with a triad to take control of the Glasgow drug market little does he know that his downfall and the destruction of his family is being plotted. As Devlin struggles with his own demons the real fight is just beginning.

There are some things you should never forgive yourself for.
Will he unlock the memories of the past in time to understand what is happening?
Will he be able to save his daughter from the danger he has put her in?

Des Dillon's turn at gangland thriller is an intelligent, brutal and very Scottish examination of the drug trade.
THE LIST

Six Black Candles
Des Dillon
ISBN 1 84282 053 2
PBK £6.99

Where's Stacie Gracie's head?

Caroline's husband abandons her (bad move) for Stacie Gracie, his assistant at the meat counter, and incurs more wrath than he anticipated. Caroline, her five sisters, mother and granny, all with a penchant for witchery, invoke the lethal spell of the Six Black Candles. A natural reaction to the break up of a marriage?

The spell does kill. You only have to look at the evidence. But will Caroline's home ever be at peace for long enough to do the spell and will Caroline really let them do it?

Set in present day Irish Catholic Coatbridge, *Six Black Candles* is bound together by the power of traditional storytelling and the strength of female familial relationships.

A darkly humorous and satanic fictional brew... with punchy directness and enormous brio.
SCOTLAND ON SUNDAY

Me and Ma Gal
Des Dillon
ISBN 1 84282 054 0
PBK £5.99

A sensitive story of boyhood friend- ship, told with irrepresible verve.

Me an Gal showed each other what to do all the time, we were good pals that way an all. We shared everthin. You'd think we would never be parted. If you never had to get married an that I really think that me an Gal'd be pals for ever. That's not to say that we never fought. Man we had some great fights so we did. The two of us could fight just about the same but I was a wee bit better than him on account of ma knowin how to kill people without a gun an all that stuff that I never showed him.

Des Dillon perfectly captures the essence of childhood. He explores the themes of lost innocence, fear and death, writing with subtlety and empathy.

Reminded me of Twain and Kerouac... a story told with wonderful verve, immediacy and warmth.
EDWIN MORGAN

Picking Brambles
and other poems
Des Dillon
ISBN 1 84282 021 4
PBK £6.99

The first pick from over a thousand poems written by Des Dillon.

I always considered myself to be first and foremost a poet. Unfortunately nobody else did. The further away from poetry I moved the more successful I became as a writer.
This collection for me is the pin- nacle of my writing career. Simply because it is my belief that poetry is at the cutting edge of language. Out there breaking new ground in the creation of meaning.
DES DILLON

A refreshing, individual style. His words are like brambles – big and succulent, whether fruity or beefy. There is a certain downbeat mood too, a weight, like the words have a fist inside them... Dillon is surely set to become one of our most power- ful poetic voices.
SCOTTISH BOOK COLLECTOR

A superb collection which easily matched his award winning nov- els for quality.
JIM CRAIG

Singin I'm No A Billy
He's A Tim
Des Dillon
ISBN 1 905222 27 0
PBK £6.99

*A Rangers and
Celtic fan are
locked in a cell
together.*

What happens when you lock up
a Celtic fan? What happens when
you lock up a Celtic fan with a
Rangers fan? What happens
when you lock up a Celtic fan
with a Rangers fan on the day of
the Old Firm match? Des Dillon
creates the situation and watches
the sparks fly as Billy and Tim
clash in a rage of sectarianism
and deep-seated hatred. When
children have been steeped in bigotry since birth, is it possible for
them to change their views?

Contains strong language.

*A humorous and insightful look
at the bigotry that exists between
Glasgow's famous football giants
Celtic and Rangers.*
RICHARD PURDEN

Broomie Law
Cinders McLeod
ISBN 0 946487 99 5
PBK £4.00

*A dry look at life
in today's Britain
through the eyes
of a five year old
street prophet.*

Named after the heart of
Glasgow's docks, Broomie Law
and her Glasgow-namesake-side-
kicks – Annie Land, Molly Cate,
Mary Hill and Hag's Castle –
have searched for truth, justice
and not the third way, for four
years in the *Glasgow Herald*.

Broomie Law is fab.
ALEX SALMOND, MP

*Cinders is a great cartoonist and
helps us to see the truth behind
the facade.*
TONY BENN

*She's that rare creature: a
woman and a cartoonist of per-
ceptive wit. Now Cinders
McLeod enters a city's heart.*
RON CLARK, THE HERALD

*Broomie's handbag packs as
great a punch as Lobey Dosser's
revolver once did in the Evening
Times.*
ELSPETH KING, STIRLING SMITH ART
GALLERY AND MUSEUM

Lord of Illusions
Dilys Rose
ISBN 1 84282 076 1
PBK £7.99

 The fourth collection of short stories from award-winning writer Dilys Rose.

Describing the human condition in all its glory – and all its folly – Lord of Illusions treats both with humour and compassion. These often wry, always thought-provoking, stories provide intriguing glimpses into the minds and desires of a diverse cast of characters, from race-winning jockeys and ice skating instructors to Italian pornographers, retired miners, and even stay-at-home mums. Although her cast of characters includes those who may be very different from us, Rose conveys the humanity of each skilfully and believably.
Each tale is a gem of the short story craft, with the surprise endings and twists of fate for which Dilys Rose is celebrated.

Dilys Rose can be compared to Katherine Mansfield in the way she takes hold of life and exposes all its vital elements in a few pages.
THE TIMES LITERARY SUPPLEMENT

Selected Stories
Dilys Rose
ISBN 1 84282 077 X
PBK £7.99

 A round-up of the best short stories from Dilys Rose.

Told form a wide range of perspectives and set in many parts of the world, Rose examines everyday lives on the edge through an unforgettable cast of characters. With subtlety, wit and dark humour, she demonstrates her seemingly effortless command of the short story from at every twist and turn of these deftly poised and finely crafted stories.

Although Dilys Rose makes writing look effortless, make no mistake, to do so takes talent, skill and effort.
THE HERALD

The true short story skills of empathy and cool, resonant economy shine through them all... subtle excellence.
THE SCOTSMAN

This City Now
Ian R Mitchell
ISBN 1 84282082 6
PBK £12.99

 Glasgow and its working class past

This City Now sets out to retrieve the hidden architectural, cultural and historical riches of some of Glasgow's working-class districts. Many who enjoy the fruits of Glasgow's recent gentrification will be surprised and delighted by the gems which Ian Mitchell has uncovered beyond the usual haunts.

An enthusiastic walker and historian, Mitchell invites us to recapture the social and political history of the working-class in Glasgow, by taking us on a journey from Partick to Rutherglen, and Clydebank to Pollokshaws, revealing the buildings which go unnoticed every day yet are worthy of so much more attention.

Once read and inspired, you will never be able to walk through Glasgow in the same way again.

Mitchell is a knowledgable, witty and affable guide through the streets of the city.
GREEN LEFT WEEKLY

Cowboys for Christ
Robin Hardy
ISBN 1 905222 41 6
HBK £14.99

 From the director of cult classic The Wicker Man.

A novel of religious sexuality and pagan murder.

Young Beth and Steve, a gospel singer and her cowboy boyfriend, both Christian members of the no-sex-before-marriage cult they call 'the silver ring thing', leave Texas to preach door-to-door in Scotland.

When, after initial hostility, they are welcomed with joy and elation to Tressock, the border fiefdom of the sinister Sir Lachlan Morrison, they assume their hosts simply want to hear more about Jesus.

How innocent and wrong they are.

Erotic, romantic, comic and horrific enough to loosen the bowels of a bronze statue.
CHRISTOPHER LEE

A proper, old-fashioned page-turner.
BIZARRE MAGAZINE

The Tar Factory
Alan Kelly
ISBN 1 84282 050 8
PBK £9.99

*There's Crazy D,
Big Chuck
Mcf**k, Mad Dog
an me*

Crazy D had planted the idea in Mad Dog's head. Slice yer leg off, accident like, an it's worth forty grand. But Crazy D bottled it and Mad D he lost his happy head - had to go elsewhere for his forty Gs didn't he? Least he still had his leg but. Of course when Denzo Doom minced ma hand with the Gulley Motor he called me 'buddy' thought I had bigger balls than a west African elephant. It was only a f**kup.

So how does a tar man make a few extra bob for the boozer? Ah'm warning you it's not pretty. Gang bangs, bribery, scams and jobbyjabbers this is some story. Wait till I tell you . . .

Unpretentious, human, moving and funny.
DES DILLON

The Tar Factory has a brash energy and undeniable linguistic authenticity.
SUNDAY HERALD

Talking with Tongues
Brian D. Finch
ISBN 1 84282 006 0
PBK £8.99

*Poetry from
Glasgow bus
driver Brian D.
Finch*

I have read [Talking with Tongues] with much interest. The language component is strong, but so is the sense of history, and indeed the whole book is a vigorous reminder of how linguistically orientated Scottish poetry has been over the centuries. It revives, in fact, the medieval macaronic tradition in a modern and witty fashion. The range of reference from Anerin to Desert Storm is good for opening the mind and scouriing it out a bit.
EDWIN MORGAN

Brian D Finch is a 'talker' of note in a city of eloquent tongues, whether in the convival surroundings of Tennent's Bar or as the accomplished poet of this collection... He feels passionately about the obscenities of modern life, composing an almost public poetry in the time-honoured Scottish tradition, yet retaining throughout an outstanding sense of humour and an ever-present awareness of the ridiculous.
TED COWAN

FICTION

Letters from the Great Wall
Jenni Daiches
ISBN 1 905222 51 3 PBK £9.99

Heartland
John MacKay
ISBN 1 905222 11 4 PBK £6.99

The Road Dance
John MacKay
ISBN 1 84282 040 0 PBK £6.99

The Burying Beetle
Ann Kelley
ISBN 1 84282 099 0 PBK £9.99

The Berlusconi Bonus
Allan Cameron
ISBN 1 905222 07 6 PBK £9.99

The Golden Menagerie
Allan Cameron
ISBN 1 84282 057 5 PBK £9.99

But n Ben A-Go-Go
Matthew Fitt
ISBN 1 905222 04 1 PBK £7.99

Deadly Code
Lin Anderson
ISBN 1 905222 03 3 PBK £9.99

Torch
Lin Anderson
ISBN 1 84282 042 7 PBK £9.99

Driftnet
Lin Anderson
ISBN 1 84282 034 6 PBK £9.99

The Underground City
Jules Verne
ISBN 1 84282 080 X PBK £7.99

The Blue Moon Book
Anne MacLeod
ISBN 1 84282 061 3 PBK £9.99

HISTORY

Scotch on the Rocks: The true story behind Whisky Galore
Arthur Swinson
ISBN 1 905222 09 2 PBK £7.99

Reportage Scotland: Scottish history in the voices of those who were there
Louise Yeoman
ISBN 1 84282 051 6 PBK £7.99

Desire Lines: A Scottish Odyssey
David R Ross
ISBN 1 84282 033 8 PBK £9.99

A Passion for Scotland
David R Ross
ISBN 1 84282 019 2 PBK £5.99

ART AND ARTISTS

Monsieur Mackintosh: the travels and paintings of Charles Rennie Mackintosh in the Pyrénées Orientales 1923-27
Robin Crichton
ISBN 1 905222 36 X PBK £15.00

Details of these and all other books we publish can be found online at **www.luath.co.uk**

Luath Press Limited

committed to publishing well written books worth reading

LUATH PRESS takes its name from Robert Burns, whose little collie Luath (*Gael.*, swift or nimble) tripped up Jean Armour at a wedding and gave him the chance to speak to the woman who was to be his wife and the abiding love of his life. Burns called one of *The Twa Dogs* Luath after Cuchullin's hunting dog in Ossian's *Fingal*. Luath Press was established in 1981 in the heart of Burns country, and is now based a few steps up the road from Burns' first lodgings on Edinburgh's Royal Mile. Luath offers you distinctive writing with a hint of unexpected pleasures. Most bookshops in the UK, the US, Canada, Australia, New Zealand and parts of Europe, either carry our books in stock or can order them for you. To order direct from us, please send a £sterling cheque, postal order, international money order or your credit card details (number, address of cardholder and expiry date) to us at the address below. Please add post and packing as follows: UK – £1.00 per delivery address; overseas surface mail – £2.50 per delivery address; overseas airmail – £3.50 for the first book to each delivery address, plus £1.00 for each additional book by airmail to the same address. If your order is a gift, we will happily enclose your card or message at no extra charge.

ILLUSTRATION: IAN KELLAS

Luath Press Limited
543/2 Castlehill
The Royal Mile
Edinburgh EH1 2ND
Scotland
Telephone: 0131 225 4326 (24 hours)
Fax: 0131 225 4324
email: sales@luath.co.uk
Website: www.luath.co.uk